W. Lincoln Dyer

Rhymes of a Radical

W. Lincoln Dyer

Rhymes of a Radical

ISBN/EAN: 9783337271879

Printed in Europe, USA, Canada, Australia, Japan

Cover: Foto ©Andreas Hilbeck / pixelio.de

More available books at **www.hansebooks.com**

RHYMES OF A RADICAL

BY

W. LINC. DYER

Ask, what is a poet?
And thus th' Muses answer:
Sensation's miracle,
A weird music master.

INDIANAPOLIS
CARLON & HOLLENBECK, PRINTERS AND BINDERS
1890.

DEDICATION

"There is among us a set of critics who seem to hold that every possible thought and image is traditional; who have no notion that there are such things as fountains in the world, small as well as great; and who would, therefore, charitably derive every rill they behold flowing for a perforation made in some other man's tank."   SAMUEL T. COLERIDGE.

INTRODUCTORY NOTE.

WHATEVER may be said of other kinds of art, it is clear that poetry as a form of literary expression is not in process of extinction. Undoubtedly the poetic Muse has passed through a serious ordeal in our United States. She has been obliged to make the acquaintance of strangers, to leave her haunts in the wildwood, to journey from city to city, to sit on great cubes of block-coal in iron mills, and to have her golden hair sprinkled with sawdust in a thousand factories. She has been compelled to travel on steamboats and in crowded railway trains, being elbowed much by the rude and profane folk who seek through such thoroughfares to enter Paradise Regained.

What effect all this has produced upon the temper and spirits of the American Muse it were hard to say; but we may still believe in her divinity, accept her work as the embroidery of a virgin's hands, and do as much as we may to lead her back from the strange places where she has been sojourning, into the primitive thickets of pawpaw and wild grape, into the woodland orchards and gardens where the June apples still grow and the old-fashioned roses are still a-blooming.

We may well be surprised at the extent and variety of the poetical compositions which our time and condition are producing. We have all manner of songs. Here is our young friend, Mr. Dyer, with his RHYMES OF A RADICAL, telling us of the things which he has seen and heard and imagined in a country village of Indiana. The book is one of many—the work of a beginner, whose mind, without the discipline of learning, seeks expression for its moods and emotions and hopes in the form of verse. It is our privilege to encourage the initial flight. The success of the song-writer, as the success of all manner of human beings, depends for the most part upon himself—upon the breadth of his vision and his strength of wing. Meanwhile I take pleasure in contributing this Introductory Note to the trial effort of Mr. Dyer in the publication of his untutored songs.   JOHN CLARK RIDPATH.

Greencastle, Nov. 26, 1890.

AUTHOR'S NOTE.

THAT much may not be expected when but little has been given, the author, with no disposition to beg for quarter, takes occasion to say the following trifles are not the creation of learned art. They are, for the most part, the product of a lad of nineteen summers whose "schooling" virtually ended more than six years before, and whose subsequent life was one of erratic endeavor. Of the quality of his verse he presumes not to speak—is, indeed, in doubt.

One day he rejoices in the hope of an humble seat within the charmed circle of the song makers of his native state; that night the banshee cries, and the day following, despairing and disconsolate, he contemplates their incineration and a vow of eternal desistance. And now, from the biased and antagonistic decisions of his own untutored mind, appeals the question to the magnanimous head and heart of the people of his natal commonwealth.

Cloverdale, Ind.

INDEX.

RHYMES OF A RADICAL

[To the American Sabbath Union.]

THE VILLAGER'S SABBATH.

"Yes! let the rich deride, the proud disdain
The simple pleasures of their lowly train—
To me more dear, congenial to my heart
One native charm than all the gloss of art."
—*Goldsmith.*

THE wheel of toil has in its round one gap
    That broken was by the Almighty hand
To set therein a life-elixired pap
    For ev'ry nation and for ev'ry land.
It is the Sabbath; institution blest
    And holier than any day or time,
A niche provided for the lab'rer's rest
    And soul refreshment with the gospel wine.

In its short space, from dewy morn till ev'n,
    What vows are spake! What glowing
        bosoms throb!
What children's hearts, and alien ones forgiv'n,
    Draw near in raptured beat unto their God!

O, day looked forward to by all mankind
    Who dwell in Christian lands and know the
        Lord,
Save in thy anti-type where can we find
    The unalloyed bliss thou dost afford?

The July sun flings down its burning ray,
    The harness of necessity is off;
The humble toiler hails this blessèd day
    In which a freeman he briefly walk.
A rev'rent, restful air pervades the land,
    Unbleating flocks, content, stray in the
        woods,
The kine with pleasant sober faces stand
    In the cool brook and chew their grassy
        cuds.

When first the purpling east proclaims the
        morn
    And day 's half fact and half a prophecy,
Ere Phoebus floods the fields of waving corn
    Awake the sire and youthful progeny.
The lark has dried her bosom in the sun
    Long ere the elder children are awake;
The six days toil for self and father 's done;
    And now, well earned, abundant rest they
        take.

The Sabbath morn 's the children's and the
    sire's,
The mother's, too, by the consent of all ;
And these soon haste away with warm desires
    In answer to the church bell's clanging call.
If it be abnegation in the child
    That to the parent gives the morn away,
Or whether night 's the time for lovers' wile,
    Or whether both, it is not mine to say.

The sermon done, the benediction said,
    Around in chatting groups the good folks
    stand
To talk with unfeigned love of Christ who
    bled,
    And shake each other's and the preacher's
    hand.
To this blest scene of high fraternal love
    The children lend an animated glow,
As 'mong the pews and friendly groups they
    move
    With agile steps, like young fawns, to and
    fro.

And through this scene more God-like than
    of earth
    With simple grace the humble pastor moves ;
All recognize his unpretending worth
    And crown him servant of the King of love.

With strength writ on his brow and mien
    sincere
  He publicly and private preaches Christ,
The youth, the ag'd, the children all revere
  And bless his kindly talk and sage advice.

To have the preacher grace the family board
  The good dames seek with pious art naïve,
And load it down with things they ill afford,
  But think themselves well paid his talk to
    have.
The salutations done, dispersed the flock,
  The merchant and the farmer side by side,
Who crack of weather, " prospects " and of
    stock,
  With half an eye to friendship, half to trade.

From kindly strictures on the sermon
    preached,
  Or simple eulogy in phrase uncouth,
The honest folk until the home is reached
  Drift to discussions of less vital truth.
Lo, in the ancient cot, ancestral home,
  That half in vines so modestly is hid,
For parents dear when they from worship
    come
  Another feast almost as rich is spread.

The children who have fam'lies of their own
   ·And live some distance from the neigh-
      borhood,
Unthought by them, and unannounced, have
      come   ·
   And wait in ambush with a likely brood.
The time is spent as well becomes the day—
   The father gives sage counsel to his son,
A mother's love directs a daughter's way,
   And through the house the happy children
      run.

There is a time for all things truth declares,
   A time to part as well as time to meet,
Hence, now the old farm wagon filled with
      chairs,
   Half full or more, stands waiting in the
      street.
A pleasant bustle 'round the cottage is,
   The youngsters clamber in full tired with
      play,
And then with parting counsel and with kiss
   The cumbrous load rolls down the village
      way.

The wee bit bairnies of the ingle-side
   With sun-tanned cheeks, and bare, brown ,
      dirty feet,

Are loth to leave their kin and with them ride
  To be unwilling dropped where ends the
    street.
" Let not ambition mock their useful toil,
  Their homely joys and destiny obscure ;
Nor grandeur hear with a disdainful smile
  The short but simple annals of the poor."[1]

Part II.

The preacher dines with brother A or B,
  A godly man, and one who loves the Lord,
Whose hand 's for the oppressed, to set them
    free,
  Whose heart with gospel love is roundly
    stored.
His spouse brings forth the treasures of the
    year
  Of meats and jams to grace their board
    this day,
Determined that her wifely skill appear
  And all the costs the preacher's talk shall
    pay.

When grace is asked and said the meal pro-
    ceeds,
  The patriarchal sire presiding o'er ;
On wholesome food the party lib'ral feeds,
  Oft pressed by host and hostess to eat more.

  [1] Gray.

The good dame's eyes as 'round she starts the
    trays
With a subdued but pleasèd glow uplights
When one commends in plain unvarnished
    phrase
    Some petted dish, or eateth of it twice.

The dinner done the dads go stalking out,
    The parson taking in the midst of them,
The "aspect of affairs" to talk about,
    And then the waiting children are brought in.
The dames remain behind to mince and chat
    And help the house-wife clear the things
    away,
To hand the clam'ring younkers this or that
    And open up the budget of the day.

The fathers laugh and anecdotes relate
    Of preachers in the early settler days ;
How Cartwright taught we'd never fall from
    grace,[1]
    Of Raccoon John's[2] and Dow's[3] eccentric
    ways.

[1] Peter Cartwright once announced he would preach on "Never falling from grace." A large crowd assembled in a grove to hear the vexed subject discussed by this great man. The stand was beneath a tree, and C., after proper introductories, sprung up and caught a strong limb above his head, exclaiming as he swung free of the ground, "As long as I hold to this limb I'll never fall." This being tacitly admitted he continued, "Christ is the strong limb and as long as you hold on to Him you'll never fall from grace," and so closed the sermon.

[2] John T. Smith, the distinguished pioneer "Campbellite" preacher of Kentucky.

[3] Lorenzo Dow, "the crazy preacher."

But by and by the women folks appear,
   A clean washed, healthful brood their steps
      atten';
They come to make and taste of social cheer
   And have their bairnies noticed by the men.

A diff''rent turn the even's talk now takes,
   The doing round, crops and such like all go,
A deeper strain the female heart awakes
   And sets the subtler energies aflow.
Wives who have read their Bibles long I wis
   And by its mysteries been much perplexed,
Who laid them by for such a time as this,
   Upon the preacher now their fire direct.

Perhaps an anxious soul desires to know
   Whence came Cain's wife? and where the
      land of Nod,
To which the wretch six thousand years ago
   Fled from the wrathful presence of his God?
Perhaps one asks, who was Melchizedec,
   The unbegat and unborn king of Peace,[1]
Who did the faithful Abram's tithes respect
   When he had spoiled the kings for Lot's
      release?

What is the sin against the Holy Ghost
   That is and ever must be unforgiv'n,

[1] Jerusalem.

Which sinks the soul to regions of the lost
  From God and Christ and life and hope and
    heav'n?
Perhaps the query is the charge of Paul
  To have the women silence keep in church—
If this applies to Christian sisters all
  In ev'ry age who for their Master work?

These and a dozen other themes are sprung
  And well discussed with reverential air,
Until low in the west declines the sun
  And night's approach bids all for it prepare.
The mooing kine now at the pasture bars
  The milkmaid and her shining pails invite,
A wakened owl hoots at the wan-faced stars
  That dimly twinkle through the web of
    night.

The company dispersed the preacher seeks
  In contemplative mood a quite nook,
And to his heart the Lord of heaven speaks
  From the bright pages of his holy book.
He seeks by meditating on God's love,
  The voiceless hymn, the fervent, heart-felt
    prayer,
To bring his soul in touch with the above
  And thus for preaching Christ himself pre-
    pare.

PART III.

The day's white heat is past ; its course is run ;
　　And gracefully the flaming sun retires
Adown the western lists, the jousting done,
　　His victory proclaimed by moon and stars.
The country lads who have no girls come in
　　To chat the village youth in the same fix,
Who inly groan and say, " It might have
　　　　been,"
　　And sympathetic tale together mix.

When Sunday-school is done there moves a
　　　　train
　　Of buxom maidens, bright-eyed, modest
　　　　dressed,
Whose glances shiv'ring through the manly
　　　　swain
　　Would light the love fires in a deacon's
　　　　breast.
The bach'lor billies¹ roundly eye them by

　　In cool, crisp lawn, and flaunting summer
　　　　plaid,
Love leaps " a conscious flame " to ev'ry eye,
　　And lo, they joy in seeing others glad.

　　¹ Billies—borrowed from Burns, and signifies young fellows.

A splendid pageant doth it all present
　　Unto the mind as well as to the e'e—
A pageantry of health and high content,
　　Of beauty, cheerfulness and piety.
' Each native Hoosier maid 's a *living gem*
　　That sparkles in the social ray serene ;
Their brothers big of heart and brawn are *men*
　　And princely couples do they make, I ween.

Though fortune's weaklings and the high
　　　born all,
　　The geniuses, and earth's proud scions claim
Elijah's mantle doth upon them fall,
　　And they our dignity and strength maintain ;
These are the mighty Atlases that bear
　　The civic structure on their shoulders
　　　strong,
These are the ones religion doth uprear
　　And drive the car of true advance along.

The coming dark its pleasant shade forecasts
　　Along the orient's withered rim and gray ;
Night breathes upon the earth its pygmy blasts
　　And lays its moist hand on the brow of day.
So sweetly, calmly, doth the ev'ning fall,
　　The fields so quiet and the sky serene,
The watcher 's half perplexed if one should call
　　The village heaven or the whole a dream.

The young man and his wife, who yet are in
   The darling glamor of their first love sweet,
Together walk as day is growing dim
   And wheel a lace-lined cab along the street.
Perhaps beside them runs a toddling boy
   A mother's love and father's precious pride;
Or, reaching up two chubby hands employ
   His little sister's carriage to help drive.

The cypress shaded church-yard on the hill
   With marble slabs moss robed, and weird,
      and tall,
Whose shadows and whose grassy walks are
      still
   Save when the crickets and the wild birds
      call,
Affords a place for those who meditate
   Unostentatious on a troubled flow;
For those who *in* their bosom wear the crape
   That God alone and Christ can see and know.

For even service sounds the kirk's clear bell
   Upon the quiet air in son'rous peal,
Up hill and down, o'er dale its echoes swell,
   And in each heart wakes int'rest for its weal.
The mourner from the church-yard hies away
   By paths unfrequent, half ashamed of tears,
The dames sedately grave and daughters gay
   Haste to devotion's place and public pray'rs.

A time and tuneless melody ascends
   That moves all heaven with its splendid roll,
No graceful fluctuations it pretends,
   But speaks the rugged language of the soul.
The lads respectful sit and listen well
   To what the parson says of life to come ;
But mixing with their thoughts of heav'n and
     hell
   A face, a girlish face, heart's-ease and home.

Soon, too soon indeed, except for lovers,
   The sermon 's done and all return
     dismissed ;
What happy scenes the friendly darkness
     covers !
   What strangely twining arms and raptured
     kiss !
Beneath the constant stars this hallowed night
   While blows the rose and hawthorn-scented
     gale,
Is born to bosoms young a new delight,
   Is softly breathed the bosom's burning tale.

When the good book is read in pious homes
   And prayer is made, in sleep still grows
     each room ;
The souls refreshed will, when the morning
     comes,
   Their toil unhonored cheerfully resume.

The twinkling lights above and God keep
    watch,
  A shadow flits across the meadow stile,
With sprightly step swings down the woody
    thatch
  Some lad belated by his sweet-heart's smile.

Agnostic vandal who doth seek to rob
  The humble toiler of this blessed day
By striking at the Christian's hope and God
  With the envenomed fang, I pray delay.
If heart ye have and if that heart be man's
  Draw near and study well our Sabbath life,
Then in polemic fields impious. hands
  I know ye dare not raise, ye dare not strike.

THE HARP AND HARPER.

ON a night that all remember
　　In the barren, bleak December,
Came a man of mighty stature
To a mansion old and gray.
Through the rooms he wandered searching,
Never from his task diverting,
For a harp on which to play.

And he found one strangely fashioned,
With a nightingale impassioned,
Soulful warbler of the night-time,
Prisoned in its living strings.
And he swept them as a master,
Soft and slow, the loud and faster;
As a master swept the strings.

But one day in early spring-time
Sudden ceased the pearly song chime,
Ceased it with a wail of anguish,
In the mansion old and gray.
And the man of mighty stature,
Mighty in his inner nature,
Found they dead at close of day.

Silence reigned a' through the mansion,
Shriveled was all soul expansion,
Thronèd was the King of Terrors,
For three days or so they say.
But upon an early morning
Spirits touched its silver cording,
And the harp began to play.

Touched the strings with holy rapture,
Throbbed they on forever after,
Throbbed they with a seraph's laughter,
In the mansion old and gray.
Millions heard the silver chiming
Of the harp strings strangely rhyming;
Rapt they listened on alway.

And the song that to them given,
Borrowed from the highest heaven,
Sweeter than a gale at even   .
Ladened with a fragrance rare.
    *   *   *   *
Louder, fuller, twangs the stringing,
Blessed symphonies out-ringing;
Buds and blossoms all the air.

FOUR LINE LECTURES.

I.

IF one can steal a thousand pounds,
　Of course he is a gent,
But, sir, if he can steal but ten
　To jail he should be sent
　　　　　　(And so he will).

II.

To get a " pile," no matter how,
　Means prestige and position,
But honest be and poor remain
　Means burdens and submission
　　　　　　(And so it should).

III.

Just bend your backs my fellow-men
　And docile take the burden,
Or they will send you to the " pen "
　With letters to the warden
　　　　　　(To keep you there).

IV.

The Pinkertons and other thugs
　Equipped with Springfield rifle,
Will justice do and bore you through
　If with the peace you trifle
　　　　　　(With aim correct).

2

V.

Stir up no fuss, make no appeal,,
    Not even to the min'sters ;
For they are busy—with their pay—
    And callin' on the sisters
                (A pleasant job).

VI.

They build a church most ev'ry day,,
    That is they build the buildin',
And take into their folds—for pay—
    The good and only midlin'
                (As we all know).

VII.

I 've got no grudge agin the Church,,
    Indeed I 'm for religion,
But tarnal sick of preachers that
    Are seekin' of position
                (And starrin' it).

VIII.

I b'lieve in guidin' Providence
    As well as gospel preachin' ;
And most our parsons b'lieve it, too,,
    And meek-like take His leadin'
                (To bigger pay).

IX.

Our congressmen and senators
  Hate sinners like a pizen,
And kick the tiresome fool into ——,
  Who 's bent on moralizin'
              (And so they should).

X.

They have no time to waste away
  Discussin' moral matters,
For they 're a-talkin higher pay
  And 'pintin' of postmasters
              (For service done).

XI.

I wonder that their heads don't bu'st
  From all their mighty thinkin'
On how to stay and increase pay,
  And from the stuff they 're drinkin'
              (In quantities).

XII.

No nation but the big U. S.
  Can grow such pow'ful critters
For makin' promises—to break—
  And suckin' in the bitters
              (For stomach's sake).

XIII.

With men like these to steer the ship
  I fear no English talkin',
No Brit can salt our eagle's tail
  Or make him stop his squawkin'
            (And floppin' 'round).

THE PLOWBOY'S DREAM.

AYE, 't is all a rural scene hereabout—
   Primeval quiet and peace undisturbed
Do spread their wings these lowly dells among,
And droning sounds of Nature, half unheard,
Come tinkling in mine ears, and seal in sleep,
Too sweet for numbered words, my willing
   eyes.

———

The mazy wood by various Iris kissed,
Set like a dream in Indian Summer sky,
Sheds a religious light and shade around.
Beneath a tree that throws umbrageous arms
Far out, and aromatic umbels bare,
Reclines a youth in grace and gravity.

His straw hat lies neglected at his feet,
His hair, like Absalom's, unpolled, falls down
And hides the callous hand his head supports.
His bosom, in the hay and corn field browned,
Is part exposed and woo's each passing gale.
The birds and sprites mischevious from above
The lad, day-dreaming where the man begins,
With leaves of various hue do speckle o'er.

His couch a tessellated spot of green
Where nature's arabesques and marquetry
Of leaves autumnal, amber nut and vine,
In wide promiscuous precision are.

Above environed 'round with branches knit
Biped musicians, the sylviadae,
In feathered chairs pour forth divinest song,
And anthems raise of slender volume sweet.
The sun, refulgent orb and king of day,
Hath from the orient crossed to occident ;
And on the tenuous copper of the west
As if his fading splendors to retrieve
The great invisible material,
The unseen world in minature doth etch.

But lo, our dreamer heeds not the display
Of matchless blending and of colors new,
Of airy forms and shapes unknown to earth.
His open eyes, straight staring in the sun
That through an erubescent rainbow shines,
Behold and yet expressionless remain.
They see but comprehend not that they see ;
For fancy tripple plates the brain in steel.

He paints a mental picture unsurpassed
That based on hope's uncertain easel is ;
The pigments, expectation and desire ;
The canvas, mind ; the brush by fancy plied ;

And to his flattered heart, hoodooed,
  bewitched,
The unborn future doth her pack wide ope.
In rapture visionous he stares into
The cup enchanted and his fate discerns.

A cot substantial on a hill-side built
He sees, and beds of tall angelica,
Catnip and rhubarb, sage, asparagus,
And dog-rose pale and vine, embosomed in.
Upon the tufted lawn and orchard sward,
The frisky calf now chasing with shrill shout,
Or romping with the red-mouthed watch-dog
  kind,
A youthful progeny and boisterous
Sport unrestrained in freedom, health and—
  dirt.

The yellow stubble, blocked with domes of
  gold
Where plump grains hide, scout every hint of
  want ;
And tedded meads that in the distance lie
Ambrosial odors lend the languished air.
The surfeit kine and equine youngsters stand
Among the aneurisms of the brook,
Where tall trees spread their grateful shade
  around
And solitary fishers troll their lines.

Inside the cot where love its pinions spread
The kindly matron, mother, wife, and all
That dignifies the sex and makes it great,
Doth diligent her household duties ply.
The shining pots and pans in order ranged,
And storèd fruits, her industry attest ;
While the lax neatness of the whole within
Refreshes and invites the lab'ring swain.

The spinning wheel with pleasant whir and
      hum,
Turned by a hand that was from girlhood deft,
A subtile under-bass concomitant
Doth make unto her simple, untaught song.
As free she sings the rustic roundelay,
A monody she sung ere she was wed,
The carded fleece in threads for winter wear,
Like textile pearls, from thumb and finger
      twist.

All this is his—the fields, the stock, the cot,
The progeny and the home-making wife.
Felicity and modest comfort here
Together dwell as twins the Siamese.
The sun sinks low and lower in the west,
The twilight dawns and twilight's even falls,
And still the youth enamoured feeds on
      dreams.
O, hour illusive ! thine 's the happy space !

The vacant stare that's seen when Fancy
    sways
His wide orbs deepen till their blue seems
    black,
And smiles that none save he interpret can
His lips, slight parted, slowly wreathe along,
And o'er his honest face a nimbus spread.
But dream, fair youth! prospective taste your
    joy!
For lo, the morrow will thy nuptials greet.

MEUM ET TUUM.

IN a vision at the dead of night
    An angel came to me bringing
A strange-wrought vase of a cubit's height,
    And the while a sweet song singing.
I oped the vase and looked within.
          Heavens!
          I saw
The happiness of other men.

AN AUTUMNAL WALK.

WITH pensive step I walk along
   The dry and sun-burnt pasture
To where the brooklet tears flow down
   The nut-brown face of Nature.

Upon its flow the bushes cast,
   With touches soft and tender,
Their kissing leaves, and whisper: " Dear
   We part. but O! remember."

Such trees as have not shed their leaves.
   The ground beneath them strewing,
Lay their soft cheeks upon the wind
   Responsive to its wooing.

The sumach dips its berries by
   The wood bird's nest, now empty,
As if to say, sweet bird come sing
   And food you'll find a-plenty.

In yonder glen the pawpaw leaves
   Lie heaped in hillocks yellow,
The bare bush swings upon the breeze
   Its rich fruit ripe and mellow.

Among the weed, o'er log and rock,
  The lithe-limbed hare is springing :
For long, hard runs when winter comes
  Before the hounds preparing.

The partridges and plovers pipe
  Their love notes half in sadness,
While strangely on my soul there steals
  A melancholy gladness.

With pensive step I walk along
  The dry and sunburnt pasture,
And with the brook my tears flow down
  The nut-brown face of Nature.

EPISTLE TO MISS D. H.

WHAT fools are men to race for treasure,
    Skimp and starve, forego all pleasure,
Just to have in endless measure
        The yellow stuff.
We call 'em " close " when talk 's of them,
And say when gone old Nick will get 'em,
        And sure enough.

Are such men fools more so than him
Who that distinction he may win
Doth study till the lamp burns dim
        And cocks crow morn;
And with the daylight's breaking in
Anew his labors doth begin,
        Mind to adorn?

Who in the verdant days of spring
When birds and poets wake and sing,
And trees and plants their ban'rets fling
        Green to the sun,
Doth ever think of just one thing,
The what to which he is aspiring,
        And labors on.

Who spurns the wild wood's pleasant hum,
The meadows where the brooklets run,
The mornings bright and evens dun
   His prize to win.
Who, when the summer days are done,
And painted skies and woods are come,
   Renewed begins.

Who turns from winter's gleeful time
Of song and shout and Christmas chime
To books that have on them the rime
   Of ages past,
That he to wisdom's heights may climb
And truthful cry I shine, I shine,
   O soul at last!

Who 's more the fool who digs for store
Of golden stuff or learnèd love?
And pants and asks for more and more
   With soulful cry;
In after years to croon it o'er,
With drear rejoicings o'er it pore,
   And grasp and die.

Let wise men with the beetle brow,
And bald head sages past and now,
In solemn conference avow
   'T is best for youth

To toil for self; no matter how
Self is denied; just ever plow;
   'T is far from truth.

Let wisdom in spectacles sit
With hairless skull and withered wit
The youth advise, condemning it
   As folly's fool;
Still youth in higher wisdom lit
This learned body knows; to-wit:
   The devil's school.

That lad 's a fool who withers up
To be with books forever shut,
And hangs around his brain like dust
   The much he knows;
A film that hides all common men,
That likewise hides himself from them;
   And so it goes.

'T is not development of head
That should be first as most 't is said,
There is development instead
   Of higher art;
It never made a fool, nor can,
But binds one to one's fellowman,
   And 't is of heart.

And who for lucre or for books
Eschews the lore of woman's looks
And pleasant words whose music brooks
          No thought of self,
Is lost to wisdom's highest prize,
And from his soul the source denies
          Of greatest wealth.

A CAUSE FOR GRIEF.

YE gods! what grief we've fallen in!
     What length of foolish notion!
When width of trousers' leg and cloth
     Determine one's promotion.

When shape of boot, the depth of sole,
     And the color of cravat
Determine who 's a gentleman,
     In connection with the hat.

If angels unto church should go
     In clothing antiquated,
The usher sure, near by the door,
     Would, smiling, say: " Be seated."

The cut of clothes, the style of hat
   Is more concern in marriage
To most of maids, I grieve to say,
   Than moral cut and carriage.

I ween one-half the marriages
   We deem so well attested,
Are only petticoats tied close
   To frock coats double-breasted.

And could we see what married is
   Stalk out of our tall churches,
We 'd see a gown escorted by
   A hat and coat and breeches.

Ye gods! alas! what grief we 're in!
   What length of foolish notion!
To fashion's wiles and fashion's smiles,
   O, what extreme devotion!

BY THE PO.

WHERE swiftly glides the river Po
    And dreamy lights flit to and fro,
Where mystic sounds both come and go,
        I wander
'Neath stars that burn so soft at night
That shed on earth their dewy bright,
And gazing on them with delight
        I ponder.

I loved a maiden long ago,
We met beside the murm'ring Po,
And there where shadows come and go
        We plighted
Our love to hold in lasting bands,
Firm welded by divinest hands,
And mine intact uprightly stands
        Though blighted.

For I 've waited, waited, waited,
As a bird that is belated,
For the hour we should be mated
        By the Po.
And I cry in all my sorrow,
" Will she come upon the morrow?
Can 't I consolation borrow? "
        But the night winds full of sorrow
        Answer " no."

Then I raise my hands to heaven,
Heart and hands at shady seven.
There I am at weird eleven
God above wild beseeching.
There I am at daylight breaking.
And my very soul is aching
From the lessons I am taking,
Lessons of deep sorrow's teaching.

Five long years I 've wandered here,
At ev'ry step I 've shed a tear,
And now a crystal lake is near
              By the Po.
O! bitter weep my tearful eyes,
Tears that sunshine never dries,
And this crystal lake doth rise
              From their flow.

Deep in my mind the happy past
Like some fond dream will ever last,
But that one joy I can not grasp—
              Her I love.
She is not of this weary earth,
Was scarce a tenant here by birth
Among these scenes of darkness, dearth,
              But above.

Here I will wander till I 'm dead
And aye at rest is laid my head,

With the green mosses for a bed
        By the Po.
Ah!   then my heart will ease from pain
And her sweet love I will regain,
As my own queen she 'll ever reign
        True I know.

JOHN BOYLE O'REILLY.

(In Memoriam.)

CHILD of a people long in oppression,
  Whose burdens and griefs from youth
    were thine own,
Well may the land of Brian and Emmet
  Own thee, O'Reilly, her patriot son.

Mellowed by love as broad as her sorrows,
  Strung with convictions sincere as her moan,
And courage to act—Erin, thy birth-land,
  Owns thee, O'Reilly, and crowns thee her
    own.

Province of Meath, no more wilt thou know
    him,
  Lost to thee, Tara, forever the youth,
Exiled O'Reilly, patriot, poet,
  Martyr puissant, sacristan of truth.

High, in the spheres at home and eternal
  Emparidised bard, thou lifteth thy song
For Erin oppressed, her glory restored,
  Freedom from shackles and opulent wrong.

Land of the dark and extended shadow,
  Lo, when thy holocaust anguish is done,
Carve on thine arches triumphant, eternal,
  John Boyle O'Reilly, my patriot son.

WRITTEN DURING A STORM.

(JULY, 1890.)

WHAT awful thoughts slide in upon my
 soul
When lightnings fiercely flash and thunders
 roll,
When the electric flame burns in the sky
And smites the temple as it passes by,
Or splits in twain the haughty granite rock
And on the earth beneath expends its shock.

When short before the blast the yieldless oak
Is snapped, or from its earthy mooring broke,
To topple for a moment, then to fall,
It's hoarse crash sounding o'er the storm-god's
 call,
My heart is filled with awe ; and fears devour
To see this evidence of matchless pow'r.

With windy yell and roar resounds the sky,
Antiphonous the sounding hills reply,
The elements in battle fierce engage
And the meek earth 's the gainer in the rage ;
For smitten, bleeding, lo, their wounds drop
 down
A salutary ichor* on the ground.

*The blood of gods—here used for rain.

'Tis fear that turns each wheel by commerce
    plied,
That floats the argosies upon the tide,
That nerves the weaver's and mechanic's arm,
That clears the field and cultivates the farm.
That to the cross the haughty alien brings—
Fears first address and love from service
    springs.

What is there in the vaulted sky serene,
The mazy wood and fields of changeful green,
The gentle hill, the unimpassioned strain,
The lapping river and the tiresome plain,
The zephyr wind, or slow descending show'r
To wake in us the idea of pow'r!

It is the thunder's hoarse resounding roar.
The startled peal that wakes the echoes o'er,
The wild careering cloud with aspect stern.
The zig-zag lightnings that destructive burn,
And the high rolling flood, that teach us can
The might of God and feebleness of man.

It is the mountain's bare and dizzy peak.
The yawning canyon and the panther's shriek,
The fretted sea that gnaws its rocky shore,
The primal forest and the lion's roar,
That on the bold. presumptious mind of man
Can lay the awing and restraining hand.

It is the terrible that is sublime,
That shrivels back the spirit that would climb
Above the stars and Jove's eternal throne,
To just conceptions and a grasp its own,
'Tis danger swift approaching teaches us
That God is Pow'r and pygmy men are dust.

While loud the storm in angry accent speaks,
And an awed terror awful on me creeps,
I turn my eyes where erst I could not see
A line nor shadow of the Deity,
And lo, upon my sight aroused there springs
The one eternal Author of all things.

THE MILLER'S DAUGHTER.

HAVE N'T you heard it?   O God!
    Katie is dead—
Katie, the miller's daughter—
    On the day she was to wed
She walked beside the water
    Where it races to the wheel,
The creaking mill above her
    And her lover grinding meal.
She walked beside the water,
    They heard her silver laughter—
Katie, the miller's daughter—
    On the day she was to wed.

And you have n't heard that—that—
    Katie is dead?—
Katie, the miller's daughter—
    On the day she was to wed
Gowned for the marriage service
    She came to sit on the sill
And wait, and watch her lover
    Grinding the grists of the mill.
A sprite did beckon to her,
    He bade her go with laughter.
She went to kiss the water
    On the day she was to wed.

How did 't happen?   O, sir,
        We 'll never know
While the stern cliffs are silent,
    Nor " waters speak as they flow."
They found her bruised and broken
    Caught fast in the water wheel,
The creaking mill above her
    And her lover grinding meal.
Poor, dripping thing ! they took her
    From the relentless water,
And heavy-hearted brought her
    From the river's sullen flow.

O, sir ! you should 'ave seen her—
        Poor Katie Brown—
So snow-white in her coffin
    And clothed in her wedding gown.
She seemed to me just resting.
    I half expected to see—
To see her open her eyes
    Aud speak again unto me.
We buried her out yonder
    Where oft she used to wander ;
A white cloud came to ponder
    O'er her grave ; and still looks down.

Kind sir, my story 's end'd—
    Poor Katie 's dead.
Her life-boat slipped its cable
    The day she was to wed.
The village people mourned her,
    And the country people round,
Farmers missed her from the mill,
    And the good folks from the town.
Her Rupert, mad with sorrow,
    Sits by the voiceless water
Where walked the miller's daughter
    On the day she was to wed.

And on each June return'ng
    Poor Katie Brown,
The pride of all the country
    And the idol of the town,
From her grave among the heather,
    To her lover mourning ever,
To her Rupert, mad with sorrow,
    As a water-wraith comes down.
And at the twilight water
    Is heard the silver laughter
Of Kate, the miller's daughter
    On the day she was to wed.

"NEAT AS A PIN."

(Air—Original.)

NOW women are not all alike,
    This fact the boys all know,
They " size " them like a connoisseur
    As down the street they go.
But all agree of all the things
    That grace fair woman-kind,
The charm of neatness doth stand next
    To a warm heart and kind.

RECITATION.

I 've the neatest little wife on this big ball
of mud. Half the men of our set are in love
with her ; and as she passes along the street
the general remark is, " What a neat little
woman !"

CHORUS.

People all say " Nora McGwinn 's "—
    Dear little woman—"as neat as a pin."
Take my advice, boys, and begin
    Tying to women as " neat as a pin."

Long years I was a bachelor,
    I said I 'd never wed,
And when the boys heard that I had
    They said, " He 's lost his head."

But when they saw my shamrock wife
   They straight way did "cave in,"
And said, "Ah, no; a prize he's won;
   She's neat as any pin."

RECITATION.

That's the universal verdict. She's somehow infused herself into our home, and it's
"neat as a pin," too. The boys may well
say I won a prize; only I knew it before I
bought my ticket.

CHORUS.

She helps me spend my wages, O,
   But that is her just due,
The strapping of her dear lord's purse's
   A thing not hard to do.
I'm happy as ten angels, bright,
   And bach'lor friends advise,
From the depth of my completeness,
   Go thou and do likewise.

RECITATION.

For besides a loving little bundle of living
excellence and neatness, *per se*, you will have
edible and digestible dinners, pockets in your
trousers, buttons on your shirts and heels on
your socks.

CHORUS.

EPISTLE TO TWO LITTLE GIRLS.

(JESSIE AND BIRDIE.)

ONCE in pleasant springtime weather,
  Out upon a blooming heather,
Sprays of vine and bud to gather,
  Walked I in a lotus dream ;
And flowers of such fragrance never
  Had I then, nor since have seen.

As I strayed, and half unknowing,
By a fountain crystal flowing,
Lo, I found two lillies growing
  Snow white on one slender stem ;
Leaving lillies fragrant blowing ;
  Friendship's stalk supported them.

Fragrant bloomed they there together,
Out upon the lonesome heather,
And unwilling them to sever
  Root and branch from soil I broke :
In my heart to bloom forever
  Planted I again the stalk.

O, ye two white holy blossoms
Fragrant blowing in my bosom,
May no fate with unkind besom
  Tear thee from my lonely heart !
Fairy queens reign in my bosom
  Bidding all but joy depart.

CUPID'S SHOT.

TEN maidens wandered in a wood
    To where from earth a fountain
        flowed—
High up a cliff that frowning stood.
They were indeed a beauteous flock,
Descended from a noble stock
That traced its lineage back before
The Roman eagle touched their shore,
Ere fierce Suetonius to them came
And quenched the holy Druid flame,
Long ere Boadicea's arts
Struck terror to th' invaders' hearts.
And first in ravish beauty these
As well as first in pedigres.
Each breast was full, the form divine,
No reed-like breadth or masculine,
And tall and straight as saplings grew
Each under limb and firm each thew.
The polished thighs, as smooth as art
E'er turned a granite shaft to mark
The spot where lies the virtuous heart
Or grace the proud triumphal arch,
Descend with slow gradations down
To where the knee swells out around.

The taper calves (beloved of men)
Gradated as the thighs descend
And melt into the ankle round
And slender foot that spurns the ground.
From hip to heel the line descends
Straight as a die and never bends,
Yet gradual variation lends
A charm that wild the heart-blood sends,
And is too much for poet pens.
The slender trunk, in beauty drest,
Well balanced on the femurs rest,
And sways in graceful attitude
Like some young poplar of the wood
When by Zephyrus passing wooed.
The frontal curve and back line straight
No mortal art can imitate,
The rounded arms do graceful move
And wake and win the eye of love,
The trunk and limbs divinely swell
And form a columned pedestal,
And it in turn supports again
The crowning glory of the man.
The whole a thing of beauty forms
That praises God and life adorns.

In dress they wore the hunting skirt
Of doe skin tanned and beaded work,
A silken baldric at the middle
Held to its place a broidered kirtle,

And from its folds a dagger bright,
Half ornament, peeped to the light.
Each held in hand an ebon bow
From whose thick centers colors flow
Of some true knight who far on fields
In joust of death his charger wheels,
And flaming 'round his head who wields
The keeny blade his foeman feels,
Who for his lady seeks the fray
While plain the day beam tracks its way,
And folds her to his bosom tight,
In dreams, amid the restful night.

All wore the colors 'cepting one
Who blither than the blithest ran,
Who laughed and sung with merry shout
And as the sunshine danced about.
She bounded o'er the brooklet's flow
As through the woods she chased the doe,
She drew the cord both swift and strong
And sped the slender shaft along,
Which leaving straight the bended bow
Was left imbeded in the roe.
With sure aim and practiced eye
She forced her arrows in the sky
And pierced the eagle as it swung
Atwixt the mountain and the sun.

Thus roved the maidens idly on,
The step was careless, so the song.
Sometimes but one, sometimes all sang
Till wide the woodland welkin rang,
And far and faint, but O, how sweet,
The echoes did each strain repeat,
As if half loth to recommence,
But fain to hold in dalliance.
So sped the morn, till at the fount
The maidens stopped their steps to count,
And spend the noon hour in the shade
That spread inviting in the glade.
Some lying on the grass reposed
And negligent their charms exposed,
Some meat produced and 'gan to eat,
The glacis table both and seat,
Whilst others hot from some short chase
With limpid water lave the face,
Or, galigaskins cast aside,
The baldric from the waist untied,
And clothed in only camisole,
With shy laugh to the fountain stole
To lave their limbs the water in,
Safe from the prying eyes of men.
These maids were what maids might have
   been
Ere to the world sin entered in.
Here unrestrained and by themselves
They gave expression to themselves.
  4

Ah! such a scene one seldom sees
Betwixt the compass of the seas.
All speak of errant knights and bold
Whose trust inviolate they hold,
And whom they hope to soon behold,
Except the maid with ebon bow
From which no knightly colors flow.
She vowed no knight or squire on earth,
No manored baron, kingly worth,
Nor dignitary of the church,
Nor scion of the field or bourse,
Could her from virginhood divorce.
Her life was free ; unfettered still
She 'd roam the copse and climb the hill,
She scorned the thought of Cupid's dart
An entrance finding to *her* heart.

"And I defy," she cried aloud,
" Thou little archer of the cloud.
Though God ye be in realms above
My heart thou canst not fix with love."
As thus she spoke with boastful lay
A pleasant youth did pass that way,
And by his side a cherub boy
Whose bow was as a silver toy,
'T was scarce a half span in its length,
Its curve could hold but little strength.
A quiver at his back was slung
Which full of tinsel arrows hung.

The peasant stopped in wonderment;
The maids a shout of laughter sent
High pealing to the firmament.

The merry maids the woods among,
To have so sudden on them sprung
The infant quaint and archer young,
And see their bathing sisters run
In gay confusion out among
The screening copse, sight to prevent,
The heavens split with merriment.

Then spoke the boastful maid by choice:
" My little man attend my voice.
What dost thou with thy silver bow?
Thou can'st not pierce the fleeing roe,
Nor stay the eagle in its flight
By setting o'er it shades of night."
She thus addressed, and thus replied
The archer from the peasant's side:
" I pierce, O maid, what e'er I see;
What Psyche[1] prompts and pleases me."
" Then pierce my heart," she gayly said,
" It never yet from wound hath bled.
How e'er, I fear thy arrow's metal
Won't even prick my hunting kirtle.
I 'll stand thy mark beside yon tree
Where plays the sunlight full and free,

[1] Wife of Cupid.

That all may judge if strength there be
In thy small bow, or skill in thee."
She thus ; and then off to the left
With merry mien ten paces stepped,
And lest, she said, 't should intercept
She swept the kirtle from her breast
And to the archer's eye and art
Exposed the bosom at the heart.

The milk-white breasts glowed in the sun
And envious admiration won.
It was enough gods to enthrall
To see that bosom rise and fall.
The maids who fled crept back to see
The archer and his archery,
But when they chanced to catch the eye
Of the slim youth who saw them fly,
Though now as usual they appear,
The eye bent down, the red flamed clear,
Which made them all the lovelier.
The cherub ere his skill he 'd try
His dove-mark scanned with ravished
    eye,
And as he hesitating hung
Clear on the air this challenge rung :
" Why hesitate ? I dare ye shoot !
Prove what thou art, and what art not.
If thou hast skill and strength thy bow
Let this breast feel, these watchers know.

Again I say, I dare ye shoot!
Prove what thou art, and what art not."
Then thrice three times he twanged his
   bow
As if to them his skill he 'd show ;
He drew the cord with God-like might,
The tinsel shaft sped swift as light,
And to the archer's wild delight
The maiden's bosom staid its flight.
He flung a kiss, laughed long and loud
As swift he vanished on a cloud.
The boaster tugged with might and main
To free her bosom from the bane ;
But all her efforts were in vain,
She could not ease the stinging pain.
Too proud to own, or gods invoke,
Off at the barb the shaft she broke,
And through the wood then sped apart
The dart still sticking in her heart.

THOU CRUEL OLD NOVEMBER.

WITH restless hands you rend apart
    The petals of the flow'rs,
You tear the mosses, trail the vines
    Bedecking Nature's bow'rs,
You seem to hate your brother months
    October and September,
And crush their pride with vengeful spite,
    Thou cruel old November.

With rowdy song you roll along
    The winter cumuli,
The wurts of Summer list'ning hear
    And fold their leaves and die.
Supine upon the grass they lie
    Death-struck in ev'ry member.
Slain by thy damp and frosty touch
    Thou cruel old November.

The woodland birds have ceased to sing
    And hasted far away,
Chased by your ice-mailed warriors to
    Some sunny southern bay.
And there they 'll stay secure and safe
    Until the seasons render
An easy passage for their flight,
    Thou cruel old November.

The rigid limbs of leafless trees,
  Clank mournfully together,
And not a smile the heavens beam
  All through this sullen weather.
Though not as cold as next to thee
  The bright and crisp December,
His peer thou art, in dreary days,
  Thou cruel old November.

You twist of Summer's leaves a wreath,
  For Summer's grave to wear,
Then ope the gates and winter rides
  In on the raw, chill air.
Your dankish breath I long shall feel
  And dreary dearth remember,
Almost a blot upon the year
  Thou cruel old November.

EPISTLE TO A RESIDENT MISS.

> "I tent less and want less
>   Their roomy fireside;
> But hanker and canker
>   To see their cursed pride."
>   —*Burns.*

WHY that averted look or stony stare
    When on the street, O maid, you pass
        us by?
Why the disdain I see for those who wear
    The thread-bare robe, that lurks in your
        cold eye?
What mighty gap 'twixt thee and them spreads
        out?
    What differs you from all the common ilk?
That from the honest, hard-worked passing
        lout
    You should, in hasty terror, draw your silk.

Is there contamination in his touch?
    Or doth a pestilence from him exhale?
That ye your unpaid drapery should clutch
    And, by your acts, his near approach bewail.
Fear not; if on your rustling train should fall
    Yon plowman's urine or his excrement,
It would not spot and stink it as your soul
    Would spot and stink it if 't were poured on it.

Were ye your inward ugliness to view
  And hideous deformity of soul,
As those who looked upon Medusa, you
  In frozen horror down in death would roll.
My blood in frenzied fury oft hath burned,
  My heart hath almost broken with its grief,
To see the obscure poor thus meanly spurned,
  And for no other cause, like dog or thief.

Say maiden, heifer, what on earth have *you*
  To raise ye 'bove the common lot—'bove us?
Your father has a dozen farms, 't is true,
  That stuck together are with mortgages.
If cross the stubborn facts as they repose
  The all-revealing ray of truth should slant,
Unto the public eye it would disclose
  An outward plenty and an inward want.

What though ye owned this western continent
  That for its milk-breasts has two mighty seas,
And slumbers 'twixt them like a youth, content,
  Upon his Delia's bosom in heart's ease ;
What though ye owned the countless herds
    that graze
  On western plains, or woody eastern slopes,
And lived in palaces?   All would not raise—
  Possession mere—above the common
    " blokes."

A rotten thought is screwed in the world's
    brain
    And babbitt'd 'round with superstition hoar,
Hydraulic rammed 'gain and again
    By each succeeding age from infant yore.
And 't is that a mysterious alchemy
    In mere possession of a ducat dwells,
The more the better, and that mortal clay
    By it 's transformed and into finer swells.

O, curst delusion! born of bastard devil!
    Begotten by same sniffling pup in hell,
Who was from Satan's smoking entrails
    dropped
    When from the azure skies pursued he fell;
May palsy sieze on all thy stinking bones!
    And may thy flesh, if flesh thou hast, be
    dung!
Forever chained among the shrieks and groans
    Of curst Gehenna! place from whence thou
    sprung.

And, lady, if I thus may dignify
    A bunch of cloth and flesh and bones and
    soul
That microscopic is to God's keen eye,
    And which to man doth by no tenure hold,

This know, and know it well, nor ne'er forget,
  Feel it by day and nightly of it dream,
In future years 't will bring thee no regret
  But joy and life: *love is the thing supreme.*

If this be true, and who will dare deny?
  Thou art a barren and a fruitless field.
What love hath ye, O maid, for those who cry
  In poverty? What sympathetic yield?
And though a virgin, thou art wed to worms
  That lie with thee and breed the broken
    heart;
And these are self, and narrow pride which
    spurns
  The toiling ones who bear the humble part.

May heaven warm thy soul's contractile walls
  And with life's essence make them to expand
Until the shadow of its greatness falls
  Healthful, umbrageous in a barren land!
The *summum bonum* of the life we live,
  The *ne plus ultra* of the life to come,
Is this and nothing else: to love and give,
  One points the action, one 's the action done.

There grows a teat in ev'ry human breast
  That full is filled with sympathetic flow,
But must, to give its uveous blood, be pressed
  By the rude fingers of a fellow's woe.

When on a brother or a sister falls
  The smiting hand of out or inward grief,
By heaven's law, by will *ex* and *im*pressed*
  All others are a corps to give relief.

There 's no such thing as men in all the earth ;
  All men are but the parts of one great man,
And make the whole enfeebled, wreck his
    worth,
  By seggregations into caste and clan.
But, maiden, drop thy ways unwomanly
  And cease to think thou'rt of some finer stuff ;
A healthy member of the man to be
  To you and me, to all, should be enough.

  *Revealed and natural law.

WHAT GREATNESS IS.

I.

WHAT man in all the world
. As brave as him
Who doth,
Contrary to himself,
Refuse to sin?

What man in all the world
As tall as him
Who stoops
From glory's vaulted fane
To humble men?

II.

Who seeks to purify
A government
Corrupt,
A minister of God
Is called and sent.

That man a Christian is,
And wears a star
Sun bright,
Who seeks to break the chains
A people wear.

THE DEATH OF INNOCENCE.

I ONCE did dream a dream so wonderful,
   Nor will I say that it was *all* a dream,
For part indeed was truth, part fancy was,
That dwelt upon me in the drowsy night.
Methought I lay in a delicious wood,
Embowered in the handiwork of God,
Itself a part—song birds, and nodding trees
Which, sweeping low their emerald branches,
The old tale told unto the daisies 'round
Their gnarled roots in harmonious sonnets.

As through an avenue my sight I ran
My glance fell on a tender, barefoot boy
Up climbing with a wearied step and slow
To where a crystal fountain thrust itself
In transport rude from a scarped cliff high up.
Soft were his eyes and blue as violet
Smiling sun kissed by the moist light of morn,
Itself a prism dividing rays of light,
Reflecting blue, absorbing orange and red.

A wealth of golden hair like a ripe sheaf
Fell down his back, around his temples clung,
And in each action of the lad there lurked
An unlearned naïvetté and winsome grace.

Then as he stooped to quaff the fountain's flow
That, laughing, leaped into a ferny dell,
And laid his cap upon a gray, mossed log
I saw writ plain by higher hands upon
A wide calm brow the legend, "Innocence."

When he had drank and from the ground arose
Refreshed he sped with vigor thus renewed,
Till coming to the stone whereby I lay
Was asked to stay with kindly look and voice
And with me hold converse. I farther spake,
As in mine own his little palm was pressed,
And said : "Where goest, child? and who thy
    father?
Thy way was long ; thou bearest dust of
    travel."

"Where goeth I !" he said as if astonished
    quite,
"And who my father? God—Jehovah—Lord.
It is not meet that I should loiter here
For sin besets me hard with foul intent
And for security I flee—to God.
Long is my way and night is coming on,
The shadows thick are falling in the glen,
The bulbul calls and night-birds trim their
    songs,
The fleeing hours do bid me haste ; farewell."

And then on me he smiled so sweetly that
Methought the presence of my God, indeed,
Was in the child.   And having spoken thus
With quickened step he pressed his onward
    way,
And I, awakened from my drowsy dream
As the proud sun came wheeling into view
And shadows fled, nor stopped to look behind,
Was woe—was pain-struck full—to find my boy,
My boy!—*mine own* cherubic boy!—cold!—
    dead!

I held his little hand clasped in mine own,
But as I slept his life lamp flickered out,
And only clay, a carnival for worms,
Was left me for to mend my broken heart.
With scarce a year sojourning 'mong us here
He wearied of our company so gross,
And in the night was led by angels forth
To wander happy in the infinite.

Rest, tender soul, in purity and peace,
Rest in the arms of Christ's immortal love,
Thy Father—God—my child, hath called thee
    home
To taste the boundless joys of the above.
Thou wert, I ween, my vision in the wood,
The child with "innocence" upon his brow,
Who fled from sin in haste unto his God.
Rest on, thy soul is in its haven now.

VILLAGE ARISTOCRACY.

"To make us love our country
Our country ought to be lovely."
—*Burke.*

Awful words for awful crimes.

I.

SAD, indeed, our little village
   Cursèd is, beneath a ban,
But 't is true ; and this foul stigma
   Is the plutocratic clan.*

II.

There 's a set about the village
   With more money far than brains,
You all will know of whom I speak
   So I will not name their names.

III.

And what is true of this small town,
   Is true of all the others,
Though large or small it matters not,
   In this they all are brothers.

* While the author believes in a "substantial equality" among
men, in fine is a disciple of Bellamy, he wages no warfare simply
because of possession. Indeed he numbers some warm personal
friends among the rich. The invective of this poem is leveled
only at those whom wealth has made supercilious, and they only
are contemplated in "plutocratic clan."

IV.

They wield the rod of sov'reign sway
  Over Church and State and all,
They 've acres broad, they 've check-
    books large,
  And—they 've narrow brains and small.

V.

Ha! brains? 't is there I make mistake!
  Such I question if they 've got,
But gild their speech in polished phrase
  For to hide its dearth of thought.

VI.

They 're a pack of apish beings
  Imitating what they see,
That 's provided it has money
  And some notoriety.

VII.

With their paunches wide distended
  But their souls just the reverse,
And a plethora prevailing
  In the stomach of their purse.

VIII.

Round they go thumbscrews applying
  To the lowly, old and young.
Though unfit to make decisions
  Loose their tongues in judgment run.

IX.

In their hands they hold the plummet
  And before it all must pass,
It is theirs to well determine (?)
  Who is wise or who 's an ass.

X.

But O grief! the cord 's elastic,
  And it has an antic way
Of contracting when the scions
  Of the rich must measured be.

XI.

Do their boys do things illegal
  Transgress making on the law?
Things immoral: 't is but wild oats
  And of course these they must sow.

XII.

Are their daughters into trouble?
  Unwed found to be with child?
They must shoot the erring laddie
  Lured by her lustful wile.

XIII.

Erring? Yes, of all the laddies
  Of a host that I might name,
There 's not one unless encouraged
  Would to virtue offer shame.

XIV.

For the maid extenuation,
   For the lad a curse they have,
She 's the daughter of a Croesus,
   He's the offspring of a slave.

XV.

If their sons by wile or promise
   Work some poor man's daughter harm
Loud they shout: " The bitch enticed
    him !"
   Or, " The king can do no harm !"

XVI.

O, what miseries do follow
   In the wake of being poor,
And this plutocratic judgment
   Is the worst that we endure.

XVII.

Money is, I ween, the center
   Of the nineteenth century,
'T is the nucleus that 's forming
   Caste and aristocracy.

XVIII.

'T is a sun whose baleful shinings
   From the central pit of night
For our grief and theirs eternal
   Warms a bastard spawn to life.

XIX.

Of the pow'rs 'mong men obtaining
  Bred on earth or bred in hell,
This gigantic curse of money
  Is the rottenest and fell.

XX.

'T is the pow'r that shields oppression
  As it is of it the cause,
'T is the warp and woof of evil
  And the father of our woes.

XXI.

'T is the pow'r that from the dunce-block
  Lifts the fool that all despise,
With authority invests him
  Over men both just and wise.

XXII.

Bursts the door of cot and senate,
  Buys the lass and robs the swain
Who doth love her with his whole heart,
  Blasts his future with heart pain.

XXIII.

Lifteth men of basest instincts,
  Who the halter do deserve,
High above the ones by nature
  They are fitted but to serve.

XXIV.

O how oft I 've seen, how often,
  Not in dreams, I speak of facts,
Seen the fool in golden jacket
  Lay the lash on wise men's backs.

XXV.

Seen the bigot, narrow-minded,
  Barricaded with his gold,
Drive the poor from warmth and shelter,
  And their halting foot-steps scold.

XXVI.

And I cursed the social ethics
  That unto a part would give
Stores of wealth, a vast abundance,
  And to others but to live.

XXVII.

But to live when lo, they labored
  From the rising of the sun
Till the even dim was on them
  And the stars came one by one.

XXVIII.

Long the father's hours of toiling,
  Short his hours of blest repose,
And the state of dreamless slumber
  Is the only joy he knows.

XXIX.

In his cot await his bairnies
  Not with healthful prattle sweet,
But with wonder if he 'll bring them
  Once in life what they can eat.

XXX.

And the mother (heaven pity
  Such a woful lot as her's,
Grant a respite to her labors
  And cessation to her tears !)

XXXI.

Sees unto their ingle coming
  Mouths to feed and backs to clothe,
Hearts to fashion, minds to polish,
  And their store a famished love.

XXXII.

I have seen the sick and maimed ones
  Who in comfort should have sat,
Battling for a crust and shelter,
  And the rich were after that.

XXXIII.

And again I cursed the system
  That such misery hath made,
Of a neighbor made a demon
  And a harlot of his maid.

XXXIV.

For the father sells the daughter
  And the daughter sells herself,
She in marriage plays the harlot,
  He a brute, and all for pelf.

XXXV.

O this practice fell, inhuman,
  Worse than all the tales of old,
Daughters bred like mares, and bovine,
  By their parents ; and for gold.

XXXVI.

And the children of such unions?
  Ev'ry mother's son of them
Is a bastard, sirs, begotten,
  Shaped in hell and born to sin.

XXXVII.

True, they specious call it marriage
  And the courts it legalize,
Marriage? ha ! that holy blending
  At its very mention flies.

XXXVIII.

Hear ye maids ! truth brands a harlot
  Whosoever of your lot
That for pelf doth lie in wedlock
  And in hell her thighs shall rot.*

* Num. v : 27.

XXXIX.

Yet, O God! how can you help it?
  If ye independent be,
You must toil both late and early
  With a penny for your fee.

XL.

And besides must be despisèd
  As a paid-for " working girl "
By the rich bedizened daughter,
  And the sensual, soulless churl.

XLI.

Hear ye parents! truth demands it;
  If ye dare your daughters force—
Force to wed some unloved rich man,
  Wed for better or for worse—

XLII.

You 're a party to the sinning,
  You 're of all the rest the one
Who to God and man and virtue
  Lo, the greatest wrong hath done.

XLIII.

Oft we shudder at the fire-side,
  And our blood is " thick'd with cold "
As we read of human blood poured
  To the demon gods of old.

XLIV.

How the pagan sons of Ammon
  Gave their first-born to the fire,
And from Moloch's brazen fingers
  Dropped them shrieking on the pyre.

XLV.

How the mothers of the far east
  Cast the living baby girl
To the serpents and the sea-cows*
  Of the Ganges' sacred whirl.

XLVI.

Had I daughters pure and holy
  And as beautiful as good,
I would rather, rather see them
  In the river's awful flood ;

XLVII.

Rather see them on the slave-blocks
  Sold to herd in filth with kine.
Than to see them at the altar
  Sold to be a concubine.

XLVIII.

These are words of awful import,
  But we live in awful times—

---

*Though now confined to Africa, hippopotami were once common in Asiatic waters.

'T is my province, 't is my duty—
Awful words for awful crimes.

XLIX.

These *are* words of awful import
    And they stab the social heart;
Let it bleed, 't is not unjustly,
    From its last drop may it part.

PART SECOND.

I.

And I heard the nations sighing
    That in wedlock thus were bound,
And the world did shake and tremble
    Like a thistle at the sound.

II.

Then I saw the civic fabric
    Of the nations wildly tossed,
For the sanctity of marriage
    And the strength of home were lost.

III.

And the nations were as old men
    Whence the flame of youth is fled,
Were as Sampson blind and feeble
    Grinding in the miller's shed.

IV.

Hung their hoar beards on their bosoms,
    Unkempt was their silver hair,
Shrunk their brows, like parchment
      wrinkled,
    And the frosts of death were there.

V.

Bent their gaunt frames thin like shadows
    When the sun is in the west,
Bent like shadows gaunt and ghastly
    When in distant moonlight drest.

VI.

Men were rushing 'round half frantic
    Seeking everything to give—
Giving cordials, life elixirs (!)
    That the dying pow'rs might live.

VII.

But in spite of all the potions
    That the civic doctors gave
Feebler grew the grand dominions,
    Bent they nearer to the grave.

VIII.

And I wondered why the people,
    Like the owlet bird of night,
Sought in darkness for specifics
    And were blind to noonday light.

IX.

Stood they like a child at even
  When the shadows thickly fall,
And the death damps of the day-time
  Like a curse are over all—

X.

When 't is neither dark nor daylight
  But the strip that lies between,
Frowns of night and sunshine smiling
  Woven, tangled like a dream—

XI.

Who hath heard some thrilling story
  That the grannies have to tell
Of the awful things that met them—
  Headless spirits back from hell—

XII.

When in youth at even's falling
  They did walk beside the tarn—
Souls of murdered maids and devils
  Vengence seeking or their harm—

XIII.

Wild-eyed watching for the spirits
  That from other worlds come back,
While, O heavens! one is grinning
  Like a demon at his back.

XIV.

Like a maid who seeks a philtre
    Of the necromancer's art
For to win and keep a lover
    When that power is in the heart

XV.

As the child in pale, mute terror
    Watched for ghosts out through the door
While one danced the goblin mazes
    Just behind him on the floor,

XVI.

So have all the civic doctors,
    And so have the most of men,
Looked without for cause and cure
    When they should have looked within.

XVII.

" Look within ! " a thousand stentors
    With one mighty voice call out,
" Look within ! sirs, for your safety ;
    Look within, and not without ! "

XVIII.

Should they turn their eyes myopic
    Where the home fire redly flares
Plagues they 'd see and rotten curses
    Toasting in their easy chairs.

XIX.

Demon chemists there distilling,
 With a skill but devils know,
A curst virus, noxious, deadly,
 That will kill the nations slow.

XX.

Leeches breeding and prolific
 With a skill above an art,
Destined to suck out the life blood
 Copious from the social heart.

XXI.

Sons of Plutus there are forging
 Earthly bondage for us all,
While their fellows fire enameled
 Forge in hell chains for the soul.

PART THIRD.

I.

It is a common sight to see
 And yet, O! how distressing,
Small men in mighty places put
 And what they 've not professing.

II.

" Statesmen "? ha! you call them " statesmen "?
 Such in them I can not see :

Asses, sir ; if more, then devils ;
  One or 't other they *must* be.

III.

Like the fool-bird, called the ostrich,
  They have hid their heads and thought
Other safe 'cause in their plenty
  They the wretchedness saw not.

IV.

And with all their " wise enactments,"
  " Legislation," and what not,
Growing is the force of devils,
  Slayers curst and addled sot.

V.

Why is it—why have the nations
  Fallen from their high estate?
Why stand they like men enfeebled
  Weeping at the temple gate?

VI.

Why is it—why have the nations
  To the verge of ruin come?
Plain you ask and plain I answer,
  Wealth has prostituted home.

VII.

. There was once a time when marriage
 Was regarded as divine,
Now 't is but a " civil contract "
 I believe the " wise " define.

VIII.

Once the maidens of the country
 Loved the laddies whom they wed ;
Holy were the children born them,
 Undefiled the marriage bed.

IX.

Heavens ! now upon their bosoms,
 In the hours of am'rous rest,
For his wealth they clasp their lovers
 Lip to lip and breast to breast.*

X.

True they specious call it marriage
 And the courts it legalize ;
Marriage? ha ! that holy blending
 At its very mention flies.

---

* While this is more than a poet's fancy, the author does not
mean to intimate there are no noble exceptions. " In 1867 there
were 9,937 divorces; in 1886, 25,535. In the twenty years between
these dates there were 328,716 divorces." For this alarming increase he has but one solution : the one given.

XI.

Is it wonder that the nations
　　Feeble are, of small amount,
When the stream of their existence
　　Is corrupted at its fount?

XII.

Cursèd be the social ethics
　　That this misery hath made,
Of a neighbor made a demon
　　And a harlot of his maid.

XIII.

Of the pow'rs 'mong men obtaining,
　　Bred on earth or bred in hell,
This gigantic curse of money
　　Is the rottenest and fell.

XIV.

Men arrayed against their fellows
　　In industrial warfare are,
Some can only rise when others
　　Victims fall in this curst war.

XV.

Mounts some Gould with pow'rs supernal?
　　Or infernal 't should be said—
Look! on what hath he ascended?
　　Living bodies of the dead.

XVI.

True, we talk with many struttings
    Of our mighty financiers,
But each million is from bones ground,
    Bloody sweat and wails and tears.

XVII.

Men are striving, souls are selling
    Anything, that they may be
Living in luxurious plenty,
    Classed as " our nobility."

XVIII.

Sure as heaven we are building,
    By the pow'r that wealth affords,
In this lovèd land of freedom
    Kings and princes, dukes and lords.

XIX.

And the idea is growing
    'Mong the people of to-day
That there is in gold alchemy
    That will make a finer clay.

XX.

O how long ere all the people
    Will this present form forsake !
O how long ere fools and statesmen
    Bury war and serve the State !

XXI.

Blessèd be the pow'r supernal
    That lifts fallen men to man,
Perish from beneath the heavens
    All that makes him less than man.

XXII.

" History " has been the writing
    Of the things that monarchs do,
Of their wars and dark intriguing
    Fame to have and revenue.

XXIII.

" Politics " has been and yet is
    In accord with notions old,
Fame forever, bloody battles,
    Provinces and piles of gold.

XXIV.

But a day is dawning brighter
    Than a poet ever saw,
In which men will dwell as brothers
    Banded by a humane law.

XXV.

And the hist'ry of the future,
    If a history it be,
Will not be that of the past time,
    But a sociology.

XXVI.

Men will study not the kingly,
　But industrial, social caste,
Then and now with care comparing
　And thus profit by the past.

XXVII.

Ah ! the politics will change then,
　Wise men reigning we shall see,
And instead of lords of vassals
　They the serving ones will be.

XXVIII.

Then the visual field concentric
　Of the statesmen will extend,
And they 'll see besides themselves that
　There are living other men.

XXIX.

There are living noble women,
　Lads and lasses, children fair,
Who of what the nation offers
　With themselves should equal share.

XXX.

Things ahead upon a straight line
　Are the only things they see,
But in front of self they stand by
　Some mysterious jugglery.

XXXI.

For their views on social science,
　　On all questions I suspect,
Politics and e'en religion,
　　Through themselves they look direct.

XXXII.

Of all media among men
　　Yea, among the devils, too,
Self is basest, most abhorrent,
　　And to nature the least true.

XXXIII.

Self is but a carnal prism
　　Which will let no ray benign
On the soul from foreign virtue
　　In its white completeness shine.

XXXIV.

Self 's a glass concavo-convex
　　With the convex turning in,
This it makes of mighty stature
　　That as slender shadows dim.

XXXV.

Falling are the scales myopic
　　From their eyes as Saul's of old,
And as he, in clearer vision,
　　Greater things they 'll soon behold.

XXXVI.

In the lowly, toiling millions,
  Stay of all prosperity,
Toilers of the farm and work-shop,
  Men and brethren they will see.

XXXVII.

And they 'll labor for their fellows
  With a holy zeal and blest,
Labor for the thin pinched infant
  Tugging at a withered breast.

XXXVIII.

Labor for earth's weary toilers
  In the humble walks of life,
Labor for the peace of nations
  And the death knell of all strife.

XXXIX.

Home to them has been a harem
  Where a soldier force might breed,
And tax-payers ; but in future
  Home will other questions lead.

XL.

So it should, for on it 's builded
  That proud structure we call state,
And their destinies are blended
  As effect and cause relate.

XLI.

Day of blest rejuvenation
  Freighted but with hopeful hours,
Bearing in thy breast elixirs
  For the withered, failing pow'rs.

XLII.

Glad I hail thy blessèd dawning,
  And my spirit lifts and sings
Till each atom in my body
  Like a silver bell out rings.

XLIII.

O the shoutings and the salvos
  That your footsteps will attend
When your mission full of mercy
  All the people comprehend.

XLIV.

And the holy heart-fires burning
  On each golden altar, when
Waving palms they shout to heaven,
  " Peace on earth good will to men."

XLV.

" Flame the fires and peal the salvos,
  Wave the palms high over head,
Peace without and in prevailing
  For industrial war is dead."

XLVI.

Swift approaching winged with heaven
   Marriage day of men I see
In which they will love their fellows
   Though of guild the same they be.

PART FOURTH.

I.

Through the darkness here surrounding
   I into the future gaze,
And at last upon our story
   See the sun fires brightly blaze.

II.

See a maid with myrtle fillet
   And a scroll held in her hand
Flying from the courts of heaven
   With a message for our land.

III.

On the high air stream her tresses
   Like a comet spun of gold,
Round her rosy loins a vesture
   Veiling half of clouds enfold.

IV.

Eyes like sapphires mixed with diamonds
   Shining through a film of tears,

On her cheeks the glow of living,
　　On her lips a smile she wears.

v.

And a head proud as Greek Helen's
　　On her perfect shoulders rests,
Queenly poised but still not haughty,
　　With a simple myrtle drest.

vi.

What a form ! 't is one as lovely
　　As those of the maids of eld,
For whose loves the gods of heaven
　　Came to earth and suffered hell *

vii.

Swifter than the wingèd lightning
　　Flaming thwart a summer sky
On her mission full of mercy
　　Sweeps this maiden from on high.

viii.

Bathed her passage in a glory
　　That no mortal words can tell,
Only 't is like on His birthnight
　　Round the watching shepherds fell.

* Gen. vi.

IX.

As above old Mt. Moriah
  Once a flaming angel swung,*
So this maiden ere alighting
  Over earth a moment hung.

X.

High upon a tropic mountain
  In a fragrant vine-clad grove,
With a magic learned of angels
  Lo, a bow'r of flow'rs she wove.

XI.

Beds she made of white tuberoses
  Laid in order on jasmine,
And of calla lillies pillows
  Fringed around with eglantine.

XII.

Next she wove of ev'ry blossom
  Amaranth, anemone,
Ev'ry bud and ev'ry blossom
  Good to smell and good to see—

XIII.

Into coverlets she wove them
  For her pleasant beds to wear,

* I Chron. xxi.

And she dipt them in a ruby
   Solvent in an infant's tear.

XIV.

What a home and what an inmate!
   Mistress and the maker, too,
Fairer than a faun or fairy
   Ever dreamed or ever knew.

XV.

From Chindara's* magic mountain
   Masters came of most repute,
And into each bud and blossom
   Breathed the spirit of the lute.

XVI.

Round it swelled a song half hidden,
   Sweet as when at night we hear
Half asleep a strain impassioned
   Plaintive on the drowsy air.

XVII.

From her lofty elevation
   Down on men this maiden smiled
Shyly, archly, as earth's maidens
   When by lover tease—beguiled.

*A fabulous mountain where musical instruments play constantly.

XVII.

And the nations waked from slumber
  Upward turned their failing sight,
Crying with a voice enfeebled
  "Abisag! our Shunammite!

XIX.

" Daughter, long, O long, we 've sought thee
  Morn and eve throughout the land,
Sought from Jordan to the great sea
  And Beer-sheba unto Dan.

XX.

" 'Mong the nations by the Nile stream
  And the maidens of the North,
From the Orient to the far West,
  Sought thee, maiden, back and forth.

XXI.

" Thou art come, O fair immortal,
  Come our waiting sight to bless
With thy wondrous eyes antalgic
  And thy wealth of golden tress.

XXII.

" See! the death damp 's on each forehead
  And the death glare 's in each eye,
Feeble are we now as old men
  And oblivion's grave is nigh.

XXIII.

" Over us the hot samiel
　　Of the desert land hath swept,
And to earth like broken rushes
　　Sink we down unmourned, unwept."

XXIV.

" Blest be thou O virgin daughter!
　　Blest be thou our Shunammite!
We, as David, pray thou warm us
　　On thy bosom back to life.

XXV.

"｡O but once to taste those red lips,
　　Once upon that breast to lie,
Then to death we bid defiance
　　For we know we can not die.

XXVI.

" Nor for once but aye, forever,
　　On thy bosom to recline
Wish we maid in holy union,
　　Thou as ours and we as thine.

XXVII.

" Thou art her who from this death spell
　　Only back our souls can win,
And we hail thee, maid immortal,
　　Daughter of the Christ of men."

XXVIII.

Speaking thus in slow procession
  Moved the fretful nations on,
Toiling up the gentle mountain
  To her bower of love and song.

XXIX.

At the door she bashful met them
  Panting from their heavy climb,
Glazed each eye, each arm was palsied,
  On their lips death's reeking rime.

XXX.

Then as blushes hot and lovely
  O'er her perfect features past,
As do circles o'er a fountain
  When therein a pebble 's cast,

XXXI.

Wide she swept her bower's curtain
  With a taper hand and slim,
And in voice almost a whisper
  Shyly said to them, " Come in."

PART FIFTH.

I.

Lo, again I look in visions
  And the nations I behold,

Not the withered fretful gray-beards
　　That I saw in days of old.

II.

For the holy maid polyandrous,
　　Living in her mountain wood,
From the grave upon her bosom
　　Back the feeble powers has wooed.

III.

From their brows like parchment wrinkled
　　Wiped the hoar frosts of decay,
From the lips of grand dominions
　　Kissed death's purpling rime away.

IV.

Lit the youth fire in each glazed eye,
　　Rounded out each shrunken limb,
Stirred the whole with wholesome vigor
　　More than ever known to men.

V.

See! she moves among them stately,
　　Wife beloved and honored queen,
Nurse who on her bosom warmed them,
　　Mother of the new regime.

VI.

As the honey from the bruised comb
    Odorous, ambrosial drips,
So a virtue and antalgic
    Distill subtile from her paps.

VII.

Round her with hilarious shoutings
    Groups a splendid progeny,
Life threads for the civic fabric,
    Moulders of its destiny.

VIII.

O my soul what raptures stir thee!
    Through my veins what lightning runs!
On my sight what light is breaking!
    To my ears what concord comes!

IX.

To my scent what odorous waftings!
    To my taste what lotus bud!
Mixing with my blood what music
    Stirs and makes me half a god!

X.

As with open eyes prophetic
    I into the future gaze,
And at last upon our story
    See the sun fires brightly blaze.

7

XI.

See a maid with myrtle fillet
    And a scroll held in her hand,
Flying from the courts of heaven
    With a message for our land.

XII.

Men from man have rudely broken
    As have worlds from off the sun,
And in guilds antagonistic
    Fragmentary wander on.

XIII.

Lo, she comes in power synthetic
    Men again to wed to man,
From this old earth to abolish
    Hateful caste and hateful clan.

XIV.

Shout my soul, nor cease thy shouting
    Till the airy ambient rings,
Shout till earth and heaven's concave
    In united sonnet sings.

XV.

Swifter fly O maid immortal
    Cinctured with the clouds of day,
Louder call to jarring mortals
    Their unhallowed strife to stay.

XVI.

Ere behind me falls the curtain
  That shall end all mortal view,
With the timbrel loud and pipings
  Heart rejoiced to welcome you.

XVII.

O to live till here and married
  To the governments of men
Thou art, maid, then not unwilling
  Will I walk death's mystic glen.

XVIII.

On thy holy, heaving bosom
  But to rest a little while
As thy son, then strengthened I will
  " Shuffle off this mortal coil."

XIX.

Once to feel thy cooling fingers
  On my tortured, aching brow,
Once to smile on me as mother
  Ere to earth I bid adieu.

XX.

Once to have thy words of kindness
  Like some wine of ages old,
Heart rejoicing, life renewing,
  Poured on my despondent soul.

XXI.

Me as son and thou as mother!
  Then it were unequaled joy
Tended by thy ministrations,
  Maid, to lay me down and die.

XXII.

Blest be God, each glowing sunset
  Swings me nearer, nearer than
E'er before the coming kingdom
  And the brotherhood of man.

XXIII.

Mother Time O bear more quickly
  All the infant days unborn,
Shorten thou the space between us
  And the dawning of this morn.

XXIV.

Then will simple plenty crown us
  And the rich will not oppress,
Then the poor will cease their wailing
  For their wrongs will have redress.

XXV.

Then thank God! no ragged army
  For a scanty crust will mourn,
While a nation lolls in plenty
  And its bins are full of corn.

XXVI.

Then the youth whose heart is hungry
  For the scholar's place and prize—
Now the fountain sweet of learning
  Lo, a lack of wealth denies—

XXVII.

Will not groan upon his pillow
  Nor the fortunate will curse,
Weeping that his sire begat him,
  That his mother gave him birth.

XXVIII.

Then the maids will cease to harlot,
  Wedding only those they love,
And the state will stand, for virtue
  Goes with marriage hand in glove.

XXIX.

Then the merchant will not hate us
  Though we trade with other men,
Then O joy! the haughty sneering
  Of a wealthy spawn will end.

XXX.

Then will die a coward spirit
  And the public heart will cure,
Then the rich will cease to flourish
  And the land will know no poor.

XXXI.

O thou maiden with the white arms
On a mercy mission sent,
Coming with the breath of angels,
Lightnings wing thy steep descent.

XXXII.

God, my Father, hear my pleadings!
List thou to mine humble cry!
Grant my soul this full fruition
Lord Jehovah ere I die.

XXXIII.

Swift she comes with lightnings wingèd,
Swift a mighty nation acts,
I with shoutings of the spirit
Lay my fancy down for facts.

EPISTLE TO J. C. McCLOSKEY.

(ON HIS NOMINATION.)

WELL, Johnnie, friend, I 'm pleased
    to know
You have the nomination ;
    In spite to congress you shall go
    Of *Journal* and creation.
The devil may stir up a fuss
    And make things smell of sulphur,
But still the fact remains to us
    In you they have no " duffer."

Sir, did the man who wields the pen,
    And guides that doughty paper,
Know you as I he 'd turn, I ken,
    And huzza loud and caper.
Well, well, I must not write too long
    As time is on me pressing,
And my poor muse has split her song
    This note to you addressing.

But when in congress* you shall poise
    'Mong legal asses braying,
And sleek fat chaplain making noise
    With make-believe of praying,

* State Legislature.

Stay by your first love-common clods,
　And teach them 'twixt their revels
The rich are simply men, not gods,
　And poor men are not devils.

———————

FRAGMENT OF AN EPISTLE TO ——.

(ON A COMPLAINT.)

THE olive tree may deaden
　And hush its sweet perfume,
But flowers where *hearts* are wedden
　Will never cease to bloom.

Hearts atwain are fragments
　From common center swung,
Love, a synthesis, unites
　The two again in one.

TO MY SISTER LENORE.

O SISTER, listen to my words,
　　Listen well where e'er thou be,
Whether resting on the mountain,
　　Whether sailing o'er the sea.
I will breathe them to the winds
　　Who will safe my message bear,
They will bear it through the distance
　　And will whisper in your ear.

O, my sister dear, I love thee,
　　Love thee truly, love thee still,
Love thee with a firm foundation,
　　Love thee as a brother will.
Thou hast left us, left us, left us,
　　Far in other lands to roam,
And we miss thee, sadly miss thee,
　　Sister dear from hearth and home.

O my sister we *do* miss thee,
　　Miss thy bright, thy fair sweet face,
Silent is the old piano,
　　Vacant is thy table place.
Silent is the dear old roof-tree,
　　Vanished is thy face so bright,
And the hearts o'erflow with sadness
　　In our dear old home to-night.

Empty is thy slumber chamber
  And the blinds are closely drawn,
Steal no more in through the window
  Rosy streaks of coming dawn.
Echo not thy gentle footfalls,
  No fresh flowers are in the urn,
And we wonder sadly, sister,
  If thou ever wilt return.

Hushed and low our conversation
  Now except a smothered sigh,
But with mention of thee, sister,
  Springs a tear to every eye.
And in voice husk with emotion
  As our hearts o'erflow with pain,
We do wonder, O! my sister,
  If thou wilt return again.

And our mother sits beside us
  With her hair besprinkled white,
List'ning to her saddened heart throbs
  And the sobbing winds of night.
Thinking of her absent daughter
  Wandering far she knows not where,
Sad her heart throbs, sadly, sadly,
  On her cheek there glists a tear.

And her hands press 'gainst her forehead
  And her breasts tumultuous rise,
As she prays unto " our Father "
  With the tear-dim in her eyes.
Prays unto the Lord Jehovah,
  Silent prays but not alone,
" Sad we miss her, sadly miss her,
  O direct her footsteps home."

And unheeded falls her knitting,
  Listless locked her fingers are,
As she flits in flights of fancy
  Where you roam in lands afar.
And her eyes assume the dreamy
  As with thoughts of thee we pore,
Sad we miss thee, sadly miss thee,
  Lost but unforgot Lenore.

And our father old and bended
  Utters not his silent grief
But upon his features written
  Sorrow's mark in bold relief.
Slower now his aged footsteps,
  Dimmer now his eyes once bright,
Leans he well toward the valley
  Hov'ring 'twixt the day and night.

And thy brothers sad and thoughtful,
  Thinking deep and thinking long,
Framing faces 'mong the embers
  As their fancy moves along;
Framing, sister, likeness of thee
  In the cam'ra of the mind,
As they list to shrieks and wailings
  Of the bleak December wind.

Thus we sit before the hearthstone
  With the ghosts of former years
Flitting fast before our visions,
  Bringing back the past with tears;
Bringing back the brightest visions,
  Visions we shall know no more,
Sad we miss thee, sadly miss thee,
  Lost but unforgot Lenore.

Sit we all in meditation
  With the embers glowing red,
Thinking of the past and present
  Ere retiring unto bed.
Sad without the wind is wailing,
  Not as sad as hearts within,
We do miss thee, O! Lenora,
  Distant far from kith or kin.

And at last the silence broken
   By our mother old and dear,
As aside is laid the knitting
   And away is brushed a tear,
" Grieve thee not my dearest children,
   Doubts dismiss and gloomy fear,
God hath spoke unto his children
   ' I am with thee ev'rywhere.' "

God is Love and Truth and Justice,
   God is Life and Way and Light,
Let us pray to him in union,
   Keep her feet in paths of right. ·
God is Love and Truth and Justice,
   Let us pray to him alone,
Sad we miss her, miss Lenora,
   O, direct her footsteps home.

These verses were written one bleak December midnight in my seventeenth year, and are here inserted because their family signification makes them very dear to me, and I wish to preserve them.

SAILOR BOY JACK.

AIR—ORIGINAL.

I HAVE waited for thee, dear Jack,
   I have listened for your step,
I have prayed for your protection,
   And in secret oft I 've wept.
When the mad winds sweep the havens,
   And the storm clouds mantle all,
I stand alone on the rock cliff
   And out o'er the wild waves call:

CHORUS.

Sailor boy Jack, O back to me come,
Warm hearts are waiting to welcome you home;
Sailor boy Jack, out on the wild sea,
Jennie is watching and waiting for thee.

Summer evens fair and lovely
   Have I stood upon the cliff,
And on evens dark with tempest,
   Watching for my dear Jack's ship.
It will come one day or other
   If above the waves it be,
Come bearing an untold treasure,
   My sailor boy Jack to me.

HYMN OF REJOICING.

CHRIST maketh no distinctions,
  There is neither Jew nor Greek;
The way of life is open
  Unto all of them that seek.
His love is like an ocean,
  Fathomless, uncircumscribed;
For not for one or many,
  But for *all* the world he died.

Earth's armies could not conquer,
  And earth's jewels could not buy
This grace and life eternal
  Which are given from on high.
Lost, alien, undeserving,
  And ungrateful, Lord, were we,
But the sun of life is risen
  And thy righteousness we see.

Then soul bow down and worship,
  Then heart lift up and sing.
Dost hear the holy promise?
  "Unto thee rich gifts I 'll bring."
O symphonies of heaven,
  O ye angels' tongues and men's,
Louder peal the praise of Him
  Who full, free, salvation sends.

TO "OUR NOBILITY."

ALAS! ye think the poor were made,
   Sirs, but to serve your int'rest,
The men as lackeys God intends
   And maids to play the mistress.

You think with coach and blooded bays,
   And castles tall and stately,
To make us feel your far remove
   That 's so apparent lately.

The mean display you make of wealth
   That gotten was unjustly,
But makes us more and more despise
   And less and less to trust ye.

PAULUS' VISION.

'TWAS on a midnight long ago,
    When earth was shrouded o'er with
      snow,
That young Paulus sat adreaming,
Half awake and half asleeping,
With the ruddy firelight streaming
Round about him in his dreaming.

And the firelight's reddening glare
Transformed objects round him there
Until the objects in his room
Grinned like spectres from the tomb;
The dreamer's half observant eye
These saw and yet did not descry.

What he saw with eye asleeping
With the brightest was in keeping,
But his other wakened eye
Saw blossoms both and dreams must die;
Yet wild his fancy painted on
For future joys, those past and gone.

Thus strange, unearthly, mixed the dream
With life's true shade and fancy's beam;
Hideous things would change to fair,
As snaky coils to braids of hair,

8

And smiling maids of seraph shape
A Gorgon's form in instant take.

But as the silent night stole on
And the bleak wind unrolled along,
His dream was changed and mental sight
Saw pictured in the dying light,
Upon the cold and whitened wall
Where dusky shadows rise and fall,
A slender hand of wondrous mold
And fettered by a band of gold.

His wakeful eye observant, too,
That fair hand saw, its owner knew;
As he beheld the golden band
Slipped slowly from the wearer's hand,
The vision faded from the wall,
The ring was broken ere its fall.

EPISTLE TO AN EARLY PRECEPTRESS.

THIS morn I met thee, lady, who of yore
　　With gentle kindness taught my feeble
　　　mind
In early youth o'er learnèd books to pore,
　　And hold in understanding tasks assigned.
'T is little that I know of wisdom's ways,
　　'T is little that I have of scholar-craft,
But still for thee I fill my meed of praise
　　And then lament it does not justice half.

Erst did my mind in youthful chaos sit,
　　A thing of life but life without a form,
Night, dearth and barrenness environed it,—
　　An unlit spark of the Eternal born;
Nor torpid it, but struggling as a flow'r
　　That hidden is in the dank womb of earth.
Out of itself to spring, to shine and show'r—
　　A thing of beauty and a thing of worth.

When thus my mind, a formless world and
　　void,
　　And darkness brooded on its voiceless deep,
Thou touched with plastic hand and round
　　deployed
　　To give it form and darkness off to sweep.

'T was thou gav'st contour unto infant me,.
　And me is mind, is ego, I, eternal self;
If aught of beauty, fragrance in me be
　I own it all, well earned, unto thyself.

And I learned a lesson, lady, from thee
　That never was nor will be writ in books,
Its only volume is Humanity,
　Its only page the gen'rous act and look.
When oft my quenchless spirit, half untamed,
　Rebellion wild, disastrous, for thee worked,
From high abuse and blows ye wise refrained,.
　And all ye did by unfeigned love was
　　marked.

As doth the sculptor to the marble bust
　The steely edge touch O, so carefully,
In that he knows to this compacted dust
　Each touch will give lasting permanency,
So you your solemn situation felt,
　And moulded with a skill 'bove hireling art
The pliant mind, and gave eternal shape
　For life's drear toil, and for its higher part.

If round my humble hearth should ever
　　spring
Young candidates for heaven or for hell,
May such as her whose gracious worth I sing,
　And who in early youth my lot befell,

Be theirs to cast in the eternal mold,
And all I have within that can rejoice
Will lift in raptured sonnet of the soul
Thanksgiving hymn to Him in Paradise.

MY DEFINITION.

ASK: What is a poet?
And the Muses answer,
A man beloved of us,
A weird music master.
An unknown quantity
Of faith, salacity,
Whose soul 's enswathed in heav'n,
Whose flesh is dipt in hell,
Whose heart is sympathy,
And life timidity,
Whose bosom's yearning love
No mortal words can tell.
Ask: What is a poet?
And thus th' Muses answer:
Sensation's miracle,
A weird music master.

THE BATTLE OF MOBILE.

THE world has heard how Farragut
   In August, Sixty-four,
Lashed himself to his ship's main-yard
   As 'round Mobile she bore.

The foeman's guns breathed flame and death,
   The shot flew thick and fast,
But high above the battle smoke
   Was he strapped to the mast.

It was, it was, a noble deed
   Done by a noble lord,
But a nobler one was there performed
   Hist'ry does not record.

The Rebel ram the " Tennessee "
   Behind Fort Morgan lay,
And bold dashed out the Yanks to whip
   And sink down in the bay.

But sheets of fire and leaden hail
   Compelled her to turn back,
With the monitor " Tecumseh "
   Hard pressing in her wake.

The turrets flamed with cannon fire
  Like the red mouth of hell,
And solid shot of fifteen inch
  Around the fleer fell.

A petard floated on the wave,
  The sailors saw it not,
And little dreamed that death was near
  Until they felt the shock.

Cap. Craven in the pilot house,
  When the explosion came,
Half through the small door op'ning out
  In hasty terror sprang.

The pilot grasped him by the leg;
  " Great God! me first," he said,
" I have a wife and children five
  Who look to me for bread."

Then thus the captain: " Go on, sir,"
  And way did quickly give;
A godlike act, and there he died
  That other ones might live.

Down sank the ship like a great stone,
  And of the six-score men,
Who manned it at the break of day,
  There lived at night but ten.

The world has heard how Farragut
   In August, Sixty-four,
Lashed himself to his ship's main-yard
   As 'round Mobile she bore.

And on our country's honor rolls
   The name of Farragut,
The sun-crowned man of war times old,
   Is high and justly put.

His name is down on Hist'ry's scroll,
   And there it ought to be,
A champion of the poor, oppressed,
   And friend of liberty.

Cap. Craven has no earthly fame,
   No praise his name is giv'n,
But it is written high upon
   The honor rolls of heav'n.

It seems proper to remark that these verses are a bare recital
of facts. Imagination plays no part whatever except in the sup-
position that the pilot's wife was still living at the time of the ca-
tastrophe. Cap. Craven is *real*, and his deed was *real*.

ODE TO THE DEAD.

REST thou O, my well beloved,
   In thy spirit dwelling place,
Thou art safe in deep oblivion,
   Locked thy form in death's embrace.
Thou art free from tribulation,
   Thou art free from slight and sneer,
From the loveless and the godless
   That one must encounter here.

It is well thy atoms sleepeth
   In the silence of the tomb,
In the mists of non-existence,
   In the awful sphere of gloom.
Friendship's coterie is broken,
   And the hearts that trusted were
Turn away in blight and wither,
   Like the Fall leaf twist and sear.

Friends with hearts as hard as granite,
   Little hearts if hearts at all,
Mean and narrow, cold and selfish,
   Rejoicing if another fall.
Tongues as long as Jacob's ladder,
   Voices loud in slander's song,
Ready, Ham-like, to preach frailties,
   Ham-like ready for a wrong.

Passing judgment on their betters,
  Mouthing things devoid of truth,
By superior weight, not wisdom,
  Crushing out aspiring youth.
Is there justice in their judgments?
  Is there truth, sweet and benign?
Ask the analyzing chemist
  If there's water in pure wine?

Now methinks that I can see them
  Seething in the central hell,
See their hearts repierced by serpents,
  Hear their supplicating yell.
And 't will be as sure as heaven   .
  They shall burn in hellish fry,
If their souls ain't microscopic
  To God's all discerning eye.

But my brothers and my sisters
  Peaceful rest in realms above,
Happy is thy strange existence
  'Mong the harmonies of love.
Hear thine ears but sweetest music,
  Never doth thy bright eyes weep,
In the palace high, eternal,
  Rest dear shades in joy and peace.

ANNIE PICKENS.

I.

"RING the bells of all the city,
 For the Gov'nor's eldest daughter,
Fair as snow-white calla lilly
Or a willow by the water,
  Is to wed."

Thus a horseman called as he rode along,
 While the proud sun set and the west grew
  dim,
As the shadows fell, and a mixèd throng
 Poured into the streets, of women and men.

II.

"To-night, to-night, by the hour of eight,
 At the Gov'nor's house will two hearts mate,
Annie his eldest will be the bride,
 And gallant Rochelle the groom by her
  side."

So the herald called as he onward rode,
 And the South's sweet maids waved their
  kerchiefs white,
As a cheer from the lips of their broth'rs
  flowed
 That shook like a leaf the morning of night.

DUAN SECOND.

I.

"TOLL the bells of all the city,
     For the Gov'nor's eldest daughter,
Fair as snow-white calla lily
Or a willow by the water—
     She is dead."

Thus a horseman called as he rode along
     Through the .city streets in the gaslight
         flare,
And the pale stars wept on the pushing throng
That on the cold pavements each other jar.

II.

"To-night, to-night, at the hour of eight,
     In the Gov'nor's house did two hearts mate,
Rochelle took Annie* his wife to be,
But now, O Heavens! no bride has he."

---

*Annie was the eldest daughter of Gov. Pickens, of South Carolina, and was wedded to Lieut. Rochelle, of the Confederate Army, April 22, 1863. As the marriage ceremony was being pronounced a Union shell tore through the walls and exploded in the room. The bride fell, mortally wounded in the temple, was placed on a sofa and, at the earnest solicitation of Rochelle, the ceremony proceeded. The poor girl had only strength to murmur assent to the marriage contract, and, smiling happily, expired in her husband's arms.

So the herald called as he sadly rode
  With a pain struck heart in the failing light;
From the South's sweet maids and their
    brothers flowed
  A moan that mixed with the wail of the
    night.

ODE TO DEPARTED SUMMER.

O THOU 'art gone, the roses fall,
    And hushed the robin's strain,
The dreary clouds droop as a pall,
    For Winter 's come again.
No more within the shady wood
    All through the day I 'll lie
And listen to the happy brood
    That warble as they fly.

The lazy brook is frozen o'er,
    The stream that turns the mill,
No more we hear their waters pour,
    The cataract is still.
The rapid river runs its race
    Beneath the ice and out;
The angler's laugh has given place
    To skater's song and shout.

The forest trees stand bare and brown
    That Summer clothed so fair;
There leaves lie damp upon the ground
    In hillocks here and there.
A mystic change has taken place,
    Their sides together fold,
In arabesque they strew the chase
    And heap upon the wold.

The North his banners wide unfurl;
   Cæcias and Argestes
Charge on the wood, the leaves upwhirl
   Among the knotted trees.
All gold and brown, and olive, too,
   They sweep across the moat,
In varied forms and varied hue
   Upon the breeze they float.

The flowers, ephemeral and gay,
   Have hied them back to earth,
Safe hidden in her womb of clay
   They wait " the second birth."
When April's silver shine and shower
   Shall crack the crust above,
Upright they 'll stand in modest power
   And ask us for our love.

The fields are brown, the stubble more,
   The scythe is hung to rest;
The rodent squirrel 's laid by his store
   And crawled into his nest.
The life-sustaining store is in
   For farmer and his beast,
And for the threat'nings of the wind
   He cares not in the least.

He sits beside his cheerful hearth,
　His wife knits by his side ;
The children make a merry mirth,
　And smoothly flows the tide.
There 're hickory and hazel nuts
　For bairnie and for wife ;
The " men folks " have their cider cup,
　Tobacco and their pipes.

The village seems a thing of death,
　No sound is in the air ;
A body 't is without the breath,
　Its narrow streets are bare,
Excepting when in winter plaid
　Appears some mittened girl ;
Who 's eyed askance by muffled lad
　Or dowdy village churl.

I 'm sitting here half sad, alone,
　I 'm dreaming of the past,
While awful 'round my casements moan
　The wild Borean blast.
Bright dreams of summer come and go,
　Of meadow, stream and hill,
Which now lie deep beneath the snow,
　And sleep ice-bound and still.

THE NEW PASTOR.

OLD Deacon Jones and Elder Smith
   Were great and godly men,
They "tended church" twice ev'ry week
   And went to bed at ten.
And all the people round about
   In speaking of these two
Said, " men like brethren Jones and Smith
   You'll find but very few."

Unbounded confidence in them
   They had, mix'd with much pride,
What e'er they said the people all
   Upon it firm relied.
The town had been for weeks agog,
   And ev'ry body said-
The little flock, of course, must have
   A parson at its head.

The one they had, a Brother Frills,
   Had died some months before,
So they engaged another man
   Chock full of Bible lore.
He came upon a Sunday eve,
   'T was crispy, cool and clear,
And half the village went in flocks
   The parson's first to hear.

9

Old Brother Smith sat on one side,
　　Jones sat on the other,
They gazed upon their minister
　　And then on one anoth'r.
At last the preacher took his text
　　And spoke quite earnestly
Of life and death, the second birth
　　And God's economy.

Next day upon the shady street
　　These village worthies met,
And as their hands in friendship meet
　　Their eyes in questions met.
"Well," quoth the Deacon, "Brother Smith,
　　Your judgment's ever good,
Now tell me if on solid base
　　Last night our parson stood?"

Then Elder Smith hung down his head,
　　A blush his face suffused,
"I can not lie," he said aside,
　　"To truth I'm better used.
It is with shame I speak of it
　　And conscience pricks me deep,
For all the while our brother spoke
　　I, sir, was sound asleep."

" But now, good friend, I 'd like to know
    (Don't beat the bush around)
  What your opinion is of him,
    And was his logic sound?"
" Well, Brother Smith, you 've been so frank
    My secret I 'll not keep,
  But tell you all as you have me:
    I, too, was sound asleep."

YOUNG MOTHER'S SONG.

AIR—ORIGINAL.

OVER my soul a light 's breaking
 Far sweeter than all the rest,
'T is love for the new born baby
 Cradled upon my proud breast.

CHORUS.

Gather white lillies and jasmine,
 Weave royal robes for my babe,
King of my heart have I crowned him
 With roses that never will fade.

Many the blisses of wifehood,
 Most holy estate and blest,
But love for one's own pure baby
 Is sweeter than *all* the rest.

Blest among women are mothers,
 But blest among them and the rest
Is she who with tears and thanksgiv'ng
 Clasps her first babe to her breast.

Others may seek for hid treasure,
 Only one joy do I seek,
The touch of my dimpled darling
 And its sweet breath on my cheek.

THIS AGE IS SCIENTIFIC.

O DEAR ! such times as we live in !
  In knowledge how prolific !
The whole world through, e'en shepherd
    crew
  Has grown so " scientific."

I 've stood it when the wise have said
  That early in gestation,
Through gills like fish an infant gets
  Its only inhalation.

That grandpa was a moneron,
  The germ of all the races,
And reproduced his simple kind
  By pinching self in pieces.*

He first felt with antennæ 'round,
  So runs the wondrous story,
Then on his hands and feet he went
  In caudal grace and glory.

---

* Moneron : a name proposed by Haeckel for a certain minute
marine organism. To the Jena professor this simple cell of albu-
men spontaneously generated is the initial or primordial life from
which, according to the laws of ontogenesis—"selection," "sur-
vival," "environment," etc., have been evolved all forms of life,
including man. The moneron reproduces itself by bisection, or
pinching itself in two.

Dame Nature tried her youthful hand
　　Upon the sea's crustacean,
And of a lobster made a man
　　By " natural selection."

Zephyrus did on Flora breathe
　　(Zephyrus was no scullion),
And of a plant a maiden made
　　(Perhaps it was a mullien).

I 've stood all this, and twice as much,
　　With patience beatific ;
For sure I knew, and so do you,
　　This age is " scientific."

They boil the water that we drink,
　　The milk that makes the butter,
And soon they 'll put a heater in
　　The Jersey heifer's udder.

But now some " scientific " man
　　Says kissing 's instrumental
In spreading the bacilli 'round,
　　And hence it 's detrimental.

Of course they 'll lay embargoes on
　　This dangerous delight,
And shut the gates of commerce down
　　On the bacilli tight.

Just think of it! ye gods and men!
　　Ye maidens, youths and ladies!
Ye dare not kiss! not even can
　　The preachers kiss the babies.

O for some isle a thousand mile
　　Out in the broad Pacific,
Where I might hie, nor hear the cry,
　　This age is " scientific."

THE TALE OF POOR LINKIE.

(IRREGULAR.)

I.

I 'VE loved a hundred girls or more,
  Some broad and others narrow,
But now my heart is set upon
  One bonnie Bertha Farrow.

II.

I 've never spoken to this maid,
  Indeed I 've never seen her;
Yet of the banged and belted throng
  I 'll swear there 's no one dearer.

III.

Just why this is, attentive friends,
  I own I can not tell;
Somehow a dream of Grecian bends
  Has wove me in a spell.

IV.

Upon her beauty ravishing
  At eve I musing dwell,
And dream, when sick, upon her smile
  I look, and lo, am well.

V.

Her breath is as the musk rose dew,
   Her cheeks are like the lilly,
Her voice is as a lover's song
   On summer nights and stilly.

VI.

Her eyes are full of unwaked song,
   Her hair 's a wreath of glory,
And one "altogether lovely"
   Is the maiden of my story.

VII.

If in this breast burned in one flame
   All high poetic giving,
I could not sing half of her worth
   In years of ceaseless striving.

VIII.

But O! she says we 're unacquaint
   Because I 'm unpresented,
And turns my friendship out of doors
   Alone and unlamented.

IX.

My heart, my heart, 't is full of grief,
   Myself I 'm most beside ;
I dinna ken where there 's relief
   Except in suicide.

X.

Some fellow has my angel one
   By Cupid I declare,
And I am left to rant in rhyme
   And tear my scanty hair.

XI.

I 'll get a string that 's ten feet long,
   Made out of flimsy paper,
Then to the garden I will go
   And cut the strangest caper;

XII.

I 'll tie one end around my neck,
   The other to a briar,
Then from a box two inches high
   Will spring the rhyming Dyer.

XIII.

The.cocks shall crow a requiem,
   The hens will help along
The doleful strain, and weep to think
   The ranting Willie gone.

XIV.

Upon the stone that marks my bones
   For those who come to sorrow,
Be this inscribed: Poor Linkie died
   For love of Bertha Farrow.

OUR ANCIENT TOWN.

I.

OUR ancient town of small renown
   Doth backward swiftly travel;
However, I have done my best
   To save it from the devil.
      It's withered up and tasteless,
         "A root out of dry ground,"
      In all the world it's matchless,
         None like it can be found.

II.

   Our ancient town to turn around
      It is no use to try,
   The thing's determined not to live
      And likewise not to die.

III.

Our ancient town is slipping down
   Toward the pit infernal,   .
But see! it spits upon its hands
   And—sleeps its sleep eternal.
      It's withered up and tasteless,
         "A root out of dry ground,"
      In all the world it's matchless,
         None like it can be found.

LINES ON WOMAN.

(IRREGULAR.)

I.

O WOMAN, silver voiced and sweet,
  With form of elfish grace,
Thou holdest hell within thy heart
And heaven in thy face.

II.

Thou art the lute of symphony,
  And discord's scale chromatic,
A naked death; and, half unveiled,
  Beatitude ecstatic.

III.

The mistress of felicity,
  Gate-keeper of dissension,
Peace-maker, too, and yet a gale
  Strife stirring and contention.

IV.

All things in you antithesize,
  All things in you seem blending,
One day to God thou lifteth up,
  The next to hell you 're sending.
And thy compassion, O how great!
  But length of tongue is greater;

Thy toilet secrets, paste and paint,
You ever hold inviolate ;
But make the neighbors all acquaint
With thine own husband's schemes of
    State—
  Thus good and bad belabor.

A NIGHT IN JUNE.

A BALMY night in the month of June
   And the river by us singing,
The rogue wind whistling his ancient tune,
Bearing and breathing a sweet perfume,
   And the white stars o'er us clinging.

A pheasant drums in a dim retreat
   Till the lonely woods ringing,
Beating the time for the flying feet
Of fays who dance to the faint song sweet
   The night birds are a-singing.

An unseen baton the choir directs,
   Periods perfectly rounding,
The grigs and river and night winds fix
Their ancient songs in a wondrous mix,
   On the rapt ear strangely sounding.

A touch of hands and of lips that kiss,
   A warm embrace and th' thing is done;
Another touch of the hot, hot lips,
A golden band on her finger slips,
   The troth is made, two hearts are one.

THE STORY SAD OF ELD.

(RELIGIO.)

THERE is a story older than
 The story of the cross;
The tale began in Eden old
 And never has been lost.
O, bow thine ears, Jehovah, down,
 And listen as I tell,
With pain-struck heart and tearful eyes,
 The story sad of eld.

Ten million times you've heard, I know,
 And thrice ten million times;
In ev'ry tongue beneath the sun,
 And, too, in ev'ry clime.
But in the coming ages, Lord,
 The penitent will tell,
With pain-struck heart and tearful eyes,
 The story sad of eld.

A tale of woe, of godless acts,
 Of misspent days and years;
Of cruel words, of sensual sin,
 And penitence and tears.

O Lord, my God, I know thou 'lt hear
  The tale I have to tell,
And my sins take as I relate
  The story sad of eld.

The consequence of evil done,
  My Lord, I pray forgive;
And grant my soul its highest boon,
  Christ's righteousness to have.
Oh, that thy home, my God, be mine!
  For there no children tell,
With pain-struck heart and tearful eyes
  The story sad of eld.

TO AN OFFENDED SCHOOL-MATE.

(AN APOLOGY.)

THE words once spoken spoken are;
　　The past is past, so let it sleep;
The present has its guiding star,
　　And future joys will surely greet
　　　　The hopeful heart.

It is our common lot to err—
　　To do the wrong, neglect the right—
And thoughtless words will often blur
　　The future luster of a life
　　　　With woful sting.

In heats of passion words are spoke,
　　The bitter, burning words of hate;
But when that narrow stream is broke,
　　Repentance comes, but oft too late
　　　　To right the wrong.

A friend's true worth few of us know,
　　As side by side we yoke our way;
The hand's not prized till falls the blow
　　That severs it eternally,
　　　　Then grief is vain.

10

While life shall last and conscience burn,
   The sins we do our peace will fret,
And hence to thee, O maid, I turn,
   And pray thee that thou wilt forget
      Those cruel words.

A DIALOGUE.

BURNS:

BAR'L ope thy spigot wide and quench
   A weary trav'ler's burning thirst,
Thy hollow 's full of " auld Scotch drink ;"
   So full thy staves maun well nigh burst.
O, listen to the humble prayer
   An honest bardie makes to you ;
But let him bow before thy shrine,
   And unto thine his own lips glue.

BAR'L :

Most honored bard, by Muses loved,
   Thy supplicating voice I hear,
And to refuse thy meek request
   Will cost the contrite hour of tear.
If sympathy's dictates I heed,
   And grant the burden of your cry,
Full well I know you 'd never cease
   Till you had drank me light and dry.

SERVANT OF GOD, ALL HAIL!

SERVANT of God, all hail!
    May victory attend
Your humble fight for the way that is right,
Like an ocean poured from an awful height,
        And grace your soul defend,
        And grace your soul defend.

        Fling the banner of God
        Wide in the blazing sun,
Till the stains that were made by cross and
    the grave
Are seen by the nations he came to save,
        And the world's heart is wrung,
        And the new song is sung.

        Preach till the setting sun
        To others eastward rise,
And westward swift flashing from spire to
    spire
Circles the earth with a ribbon of fire
        Holy to angel eyes,
        Holy to angel eyes.

        Preach the kingship of Christ
        With unction from on high,

Till matin devotions follow the sun
And back to the pray'r of the even come,
  Kissing each other good-night,
  Kissing each other good-night.

  Thunder the wrath of God
  On " folly as it flies,"
Preach of the place where the agonized tear
Shall fall till the soul of the weeper appear
  Stainless to heav'nly eyes,
  Precious to heav'nly eyes.

  Preach the home of the soul
  Where pious pilgrims go,
Where dwellers ne'er know the feeling of pain
Nor onto the cheek e'er cometh a stain
  Made by the lachrymal flow,
  Made by the lachrymal flow.

  Servant of God, all hail!
  May victory attend
Your humble fight for the way that is right,
Like an ocean poured from an awful height,
  And grace your soul defend,
  And grace your soul defend.

MY MARIA.

(AIR—ORIGINAL.)

NOT for the freshness of her face,
  Nor the fullness of her purse,
Did I wed my lost Maria,
  Wed for better or for worse.
Sprightly was she when a maiden,
  And her lands were rich and broad,
Still I wed not face nor fortune,
  But the soul of her I loved.
Joined were we in holy union,
  Not in form nor all in name,
But as Inspiration teaches,
  One in substance and the same.

CHORUS.

My Maria, loved Maria,
  'Neath the green-wood tree,
Sings the river on forever
  Requiems for thee.
My Maria, loved Maria,
  Sainted shade in light,
Thy death severed two fond hearts, love,
  Mine will them unite.

Fifty years we walked in gladness,
　　Living in each other's life,
I was loved and honored husband,
　　She was loved and honored wife ;
Love like hers knows of no limit
　　Bending to the human will,
For besides her own she sought to
　　Swing my burdens up life's hill.
O my lost, my loved Maria,
　　I am waiting for the day,
When to thee from earth and anguish
　　Swift shall speed my soul away.

IT BUDS BUT BLOSSOMS NEVER.

I.

ONE-HALF of nature's numbers sweet,
　　Unloved, unheard, fall at my feet ;
And to myself I do repeat,
　　　　Over and o'er,
　　　　Over and o'er,
What cause hast thou, O heart, for grief,
　　　　Than others more,
　　　　Than others more.

II.

Within my soul there buds a flower;
'Twas planted in an early hour,
And nourished by youth's shine and shower,
  So warm and sweet,
  So warm and sweet;
And from this soil no mortal power
  Can pluck its feet,
  Can pluck its feet.
Though it buds it blossoms never;
Though it dies it lives forever;
Though it lives 't is dying ever
  Within my heart,
  Within my heart;
Though I could I would not sever
  It from my heart,
  It from my heart.

A LITTLE BOY'S SOLILOQUY.

I NOW am but a little boy ;
  To be a man I 'll grow,
And out among (to think what joy !)
  The pretty maids I 'll go.

I 'll have just lots and lots of fun
  Each night and every day ;
I 'll labor, too ; it must be done ;
  There's work as well as play.

Some day I 'll wed a neighbor girl
  That can make bread and pies ;
Who 's fond of work, who wears a curl,
  And loves me well besides.

We 'll build a house, and live in it ;
  And O what jolly fun
Upon the portico to sit,
  Like pa, when work is done.

I now am but a boy, I know ;
  Some day I 'll be a man ;
And those who laugh I then will show
  That do these things I can.

VALEDICTION.

BROTHER, be not faint, despondent,
  Strong be thou and hope alway,
Sink not down thy cares bemoaning
  Overburdened by the way.

Does another move beside thee
  Burdened with a load of care?
Though thine own is twice the greater,
  Share it brother, brother share.

All the grief we bear for others,
  All their burdens that we take,
Toiling on life's dusty highway,
  Will our own the lighter make.

Kindly speak to this and that one,
  Words of comfort and of cheer;
Words of courage, calm and trustful
  Fall like balm upon the ear.

Nor but speak in words of kindness,
  Doing is of love the sum,
And I tell thee truly, brother,
  Actions speak when words are dumb.

By an act, a good example,
  By the tribute of a smile,
We may wake a latent goodness
  Flowing dormant all the while.

We may dissipate a storm cloud,
  Generate a hope sublime,
By a word of kind advisement
  Spoken in the nick of time.

Brother, be not faint, despondent.
  Strong be thou and hope alway,
Sink not down by cares bemoaning
  Overburdened by the way.

Plate thy breast with trust in heaven,
  Let hope's banner be unfurled,
Blazoned with a promised mansion
  In that holy deathless world.